BECAUSE OF THE SUN

BECAUSE OF THE SUN

JENNY TORRES SANCHEZ

DELACORTE PRESS

Text copyright © 2017 by Jenny Torres Sanchez
Jacket art copyright © 2017 by Anne Jordan and Mitch Goldstein

All rights reserved. Published in the United States by Delacorte Press, an imprint of Random House Children's Books, a division of Penguin Random House LLC, New York.

Delacorte Press is a registered trademark and the colophon is a trademark of Penguin Random House LLC.

Visit us on the Web! randomhouseteens.com

Educators and librarians, for a variety of teaching tools, visit us at RHTeachersLibrarians.com

Library of Congress Cataloging-in-Publication Data
Names: Torres Sanchez, Jenny, author.
Title: Because of the sun / Jenny Torres Sanchez.
Description: New York : Delacorte Press, [2017] | Summary: Seventeen-year-old Dani struggles with how to process the ambiguous grief she feels in the aftermath of her mother's death after moving to New Mexico with an aunt she never met.
Identifiers: LCCN 2015050826 (print) | LCCN 2016024855 (ebook) | ISBN 978-0-399-55145-1 (trade hardcover) | ISBN 978-0-399-55146-8 (library binding) | ISBN 978-0-399-55148-2 (ebook) | ISBN 978-1-5247-1913-5 (intl. tr. pbk.)
Subjects: | CYAC: Grief—Fiction. | Mothers and daughters—Fiction. | Family Problems—Fiction. | Aunts—Fiction. | Orphans—Fiction.
Classification: LCC PZ7.T6457245 Bec 2017 (print) | LCC PZ7.T6457245 (ebook) | DDC [Fic]—dc23

The text of this book is set in 12-point Berling.
Interior design by Trish Parcell

Printed in the United States of America
10 9 8 7 6 5 4 3 2 1
First Edition

Para mis queridos padres,

Miriam y David

CONTENTS

PART ONE

What I remember is the shell-pink nail polish. Even as I looked at it, her pinky finger dangling with that frosty color, I wondered, *Why this? Why am I noticing this?*

It's strange how your mind can split into so many different bits and pieces, slivers of it sending a thousand different messages. *Scream. Run.* Or *Careful, careful, don't startle the bear.* Other parts recall a television show about worst-case scenarios that tell you *Don't make eye contact, play dead,* even as your lungs send a distress signal and your brain reminds you to *Breathe.*

Now a part insists *She's dead. Look at the blood.* Another insists *She can't be.* Another laughs at the absurdity and assures you *Don't worry, none of this is real.*

And then there's the part that registers shell-pink nail polish. *Delicate and pretty and coating her nails perfectly, making them look like seashells.* You can hardly take your eyes off it, even as another part takes in

her dangling pinky,
the look on her face,
how her body is sprawled out,
the pink of the pool water,
and the bear . . .

She asked me if I wanted to sit out near the pool
with her and I didn't. I told her it was too hot, and
besides it was the last two weeks of school and I had
end-of-year exams to study for. But she didn't even
let me finish before she started shaking her head and
talking over me. *God, Dani. Have some fucking fun for
once, would you?* she said as she splashed some vodka
into her lemonade.

But I *did* have exams. And it *was* too hot. It was
always too hot. And even if it wasn't officially summer yet, it was always summer in Florida, the sun was
always blinding, and we, me and her, we were always
like this. I couldn't think of a worse way to spend
the afternoon than with my mother, telling me all the
ways I was stunted or terrible or not like her.

I looked at her from the corner of my eye, taking
in another of her barely there bikinis and too-tan skin.

"You're going to get skin cancer," I told her because
I couldn't help myself.

She laughed, shook her head. "Well, we all die of
something, Dani. Who the hell cares if it's skin cancer
or something else." She took a sip of her drink, then
flipped her long blond hair with hardly a glance in
my direction, the way she always did when she was

done with me. When she couldn't care less what I said next.

I don't know why I hated her. Or I do know, but the reasons, they don't translate to words. All I know is she made it hard to breathe, and a tightness would shoot across my chest, from one shoulder to another, and press down on me. And somehow I hated myself. Just because I was her daughter. Her terrible daughter, as she liked to remind me.

I watched her open the sliding glass door that led to the pool and the patio and then close it behind her. I watched her untie her top and lie down on her stomach, taking her time to get comfortable even though the yard wasn't fenced in. Even though the neighbors on either side could look out and see her and often did. She knew it, too. She reveled in it.

I watched her. I watched every move she made. And I thought, *I'll never be like you.*

I waited to see if you would look at me. But you closed your eyes.

One of my tests she always failed.

So I went to my room, that empty, self-satisfied feeling enveloping me in a cloud of self-hatred. *Because, oh, how you made me hate myself. You made me want to cover up from head to toe, wish to be anything but your daughter.* I flopped on my bed, pulling out from under me notes and study guides that were now useless *because my head was too full with you. With anger and rage for you. With how you shoved your way into my every thought when all I wanted was to get away from you.*

I plugged in my headphones. Turned the music up so loud it hurt my head and left no room for you. Turned it up so I could be anywhere but there. Turned it up so I'd forget about school and you half-dressed in the backyard for all the world to see.

I guess that's why I didn't hear you screaming.

• • •

I stay with our neighbor Helen. Helen is odd but nice. She's maybe forty and lives alone. Her eyes are small, impossible to read, and her face is so pale and doughy that her expressions seem to melt into each other until there's just one—a mixture of complacency and boredom.

She tried to be Mom's friend, but Mom didn't pay much attention to her. Helen doesn't wear bikinis or attract men.

Helen told the child services lady that I can stay with her until they figure out what to do with me. I told the child services lady *I can take care of myself. I've always taken care of myself. I'm almost eighteen,* but she looked at me like she didn't understand what I was saying. So I finally said *Yeah, I'll stay with Helen.* In fact, I told her, I always stayed with Helen because Helen and Mom were best friends. I don't know why I said that. But Helen just nodded and the lady agreed.

6

I'm glad. Especially with so many television cameras outside, and trappers looking for the black bear that came for Mom. They search for him like he's a serial killer. People are told to stay inside. Nobody lies out in the sun like she did. Nobody ever did, anyway. The night is filled with the flashing lights of police cars and black trucks roaming the streets.

But I am safe in Helen's stuffy little house. I like the way it closes in around me, holding me down. I like being somewhere unfamiliar, under so many thick blankets and pillows that smell like dust, where no one can find me. I pretend I'm a bug that can go unnoticed. I almost wish I'd wake up as an insect, with no memory of my human self.

But my brain betrays me. It keeps flashing, short-circuiting. It keeps zapping me with electricity.

I see myself coming downstairs and looking out the sliding glass door. I didn't even scream. But the bear saw me anyway, and for a moment, I thought he would charge. Instead he just turned and walked off.

There were a few neighbors who came out, trying to distract him. Old and frail Mr. Sterling, banging on a pot, half his body out the door, the other half inside, guarding Mrs. Sterling, who watched with her hand to her mouth, ready to retreat and slam the door if necessary. And the man who lived two houses down from us, who washed his car when you did, and his son, home from college, I guess. They both ran to you when the bear finally turned and left. They yelled something at me and I tried to understand but I couldn't make sense of the sounds coming from their mouths. I just stood there, because of that part of my brain telling me none of it was real anyway.

Not your exposed breasts.

Not the blood.

None of it.

If you hadn't just been mauled, you would have enjoyed the attention.

My brain zaps. And now I see how *you smile at a man standing over you. You touch his cheek; your nails against his skin. And you wrap your arms around his neck and tell him you love him. Then you kiss him.*

Electricity fills my body and mind and I wonder if this is what it feels like to be struck by lightning. I wonder if I can be zapped enough to burn all the memories.

Then there you are again, *standing by the pool.*

This time there is no bear.

No neighbors.

Nothing.

Just you. Looking at the sky. Your throat throbbing with a silent scream.

Why are you screaming?

I see my reflection in the glass door and I think, *That girl doesn't exist.* And I'm zapped again and it is dark and I am the girl in Helen's house trying to piece her brain back together. Choosing which parts I will keep. Which parts I can do without.

The part that tells me it never happened is the part I like best.

It was some other mother. Some other girl. Not you. You've never had a mother. You've always been on your own. Big deal. There are so many orphans in the world.

Right.

That's all. I'm just another orphan who has no idea who her parents were.

That's the best way to think about it. I don't even feel sorry for myself.

What makes me so special anyway?

• • •

The cameras leave in the morning but return two days later, in the blazing-hot afternoon, because the black bear has been captured. I watch the reporters and cameras from Helen's living room, from behind sheer white curtains. One reporter's shirt is damp, stained with wet spots on the back.

Two hours later, I see that reporter on the television, the house we lived in and Helen's house in the background. His face is glistening as he announces that the bear will be euthanized.

I focus on the window behind him. I watch the white curtains I was standing behind move ever so slightly. I am there. And I laugh because I am everywhere.

On the couch.

Behind the curtains.

In the television.

Then the reporter is wearing different clothes. I wonder how he changed so quickly, but realize I'm in another day, watching another report, a follow-up to *that horrific story we brought you earlier this week about the black bear that killed a woman in her own backyard.*

The camera pans our front yard, showing animal rights activists who are picketing and holding up signs that read SAVE THE BEAR! IT'S NOT HIS FAULT!

I study their hot, angry faces.

Whose fault is it? I ask them.

But the activists just hold their signs up higher.

Not his! they say.

I get up and look out the front window but nobody is there. I click off the television and settle back on the couch, where I stare at the black screen until darkness fills my head and sleep takes over. I feel far away, but I see myself right there on Helen's couch. I see the television buzz to life again.

This time the bear is on the screen, with handcuffs and chains around his paws. I see guards leading him down a long hall to a room.

Dead bear walking!

He could overpower both guards in seconds, disembowel them with a swipe of one paw. But he is calm. He allows them to strap him to a white cot. They watch the clock. No phones ring.

He turns his head and looks at me with his two great glistening eyes.

But I won't look in his eyes. I look at his paws, bristly and leathery.

They administer the first injection. Then a second one. And then he closes his eyes and lets out a low groan as they push in the third.

A vet enters, listens for a heartbeat. He nods and they pull a white sheet over the bear. Someone draws a curtain closed on one side of the television. Then the other. And there is only a black screen again.

I go to sleep that night in the same room at Helen's, the one that smells of old dust and salty skin and feels both strange and familiar. I dream I am the vet at the execution. But every time I listen for the bear's heartbeat, I can still hear it, thumping loudly. They give him a fourth, a fifth, a sixth injection. Still it beats on.

The straps on his limbs dissolve as I listen again.

He reaches up and caresses my hair.

Shhhhhhhh, he says. *Shhhhhhhh.*

I almost believe he's sorry.

But then I'm scared. Because his soft whisper sounds like waking up in the middle of the night and realizing darkness has limbs and teeth; darkness breathes and is standing over you, ready to put his heavy paw over your mouth.

Play dead, my brain commands.

• • •

On one of these nights, as I lie in my room at Helen's, I remember there are exams and bubbles and blank pages waiting to be filled with my No. 2 pencil. I decide I'm tired of the reporter and his sweat-stained shirt.

The next morning, I wake up early and go to my house to get ready for school. The street is deserted and dark when I step outside, so I almost don't see the guy sitting on his motorcycle until he calls out to me.

"Hey, kid," he says. I don't think he knows my name. I've only really talked to him a few times, but he was Mom's latest boyfriend. My brain does something funny with the word *latest*. Black marks slash out the middle *t* and *e*. Her last.

I walk over to him because I don't know what else to do. Maybe he forgot something here and came back to get it.

He takes out a cigarette, offers me one. I shake my head.

He stares at the house. "I was out, hanging with some buddies tonight, and then everyone went home. And I started this way, you know, before I remembered." He looks at me like I should feel sorry for him. "I'd forgotten. Isn't that crazy? Nearly ran off the road, into a tree, when I remembered. But I couldn't turn back, something wouldn't let me, so I just kept going. Anyway, here I am." He looks at the house, then at me, like I should know what to do. Like I can go inside and tell her he's here and watch her put on lipstick and rush about, only to lean against the front door the way she would, pretending she didn't care.

"Good woman . . ." He shakes his head, takes a deep breath, lets it out slowly.

I think he was the one who paid for the funeral. I think he was the one who arranged it all. I don't know. He's a pseudo biker, has an office day job; I know that much. Mom once said he wasn't a "real" biker, but he would do for now. I almost feel like telling him *She was just using you. And you were just using her, right? But at some point she would've thought she loved you and she would've begged you to stay. But you wouldn't have. Because she can't hide who she is forever.*

"You all right?" he asks, as if suddenly remembering she was my mother. Then he gives me a funny look. "Wait. Are you staying here?"

I shake my head. "With a neighbor." My voice sounds funny and I wonder when I last spoke.

"Oh," he says, nodding. He searches his pockets and takes out some money. "Here," he says, pressing a bunch of bills into my hand. "Take this. In case you need anything."

I stare at the money, a neat roll of bills, like the ones Mom had at the beginning of each month for the last few months. I don't want to take it. I don't want to be like her, but it sits in my palm as he starts up his bike with a roar and says, "Anyway, I gotta go. You take

13

care of yourself." He tips his head in my direction, revs the engine, and maneuvers the bike away from me. I watch him ride off, the red lights still bright in the dark before dawn.

A part of me panics, wants to run after him and yell *Wait, don't go! I can't stay with Helen forever! What do I do?* But I force myself to stand still, silent, as I watch him speed down the road. And I laugh, reminding myself *You don't even know his name.*

Tom. I think his name was Tom.

I go to my house and quickly get ready. That's what I tell myself, anyway. *Get ready quickly.* But my eyes notice the vodka bottle on the counter where she left it, and for a minute, I think maybe if she'd been sober, she would've known what to do.

You play dead.

I notice a pair of her shorts on the couch, flimsy, bright shorts she got in the teen section of Walmart. Shorts I'd never wear.

I remember this movie I saw once, where some woman's mother died. And the daughter goes to the closet and smells her clothes. Takes big, deep breaths of her mother's scent.

I zip up my jeans. I put on socks. I grab a sweater I don't need.

I won't go in her room. I won't go in there and take deep huffs of sex. Of vodka and thick perfume. I won't go into her bathroom, where she kept a basket full of bright nail polish on the counter. I won't search for the shell-pink she must have bought *when? Why?* I won't carry it with me.

I won't think of her.

If you took all that away, what would she have smelled like?

In the movie, the daughter cries as she holds a piece of her mother's clothing to her chest, like she's bleeding and this shirt or blouse or something is stopping the blood from spilling all over the floor.

I tell my brain it is stupid. I push that thought away. Because that wasn't my mother. And I wasn't that daughter.

I leave all the lights off, except the one in my room. I don't want to see anything else. I head back to Helen's.

"You sure?" Helen asks when I tell her I'm going to school and she sees my backpack slung over my shoulder. She doesn't think I should go.

"Why not?"

"I don't know," she says. She's eating microwave pizza for breakfast. "Just didn't figure you'd go."

"What else would I do?" I ask her. She shrugs and takes another bite of her pizza.

But I'm serious. What else would I do? I can't think of a single other thing I could do. I can't even remember what I've been doing. Days have passed and I forget them as soon as I think about them too hard.

I finish cereal I don't remember pouring and head outside.

The sun is unbearably hot as I walk to the bus stop. Others are already there, but they stop talking when they see me.

Nobody talks to you when your mother has been mauled to death by a bear. Not that they talked to me before. No, they don't talk to me, but they look at me. They look at me the way their moms looked at my mom. They turn their heads and whisper to each other. But I see the words, big, blocky, black-lettered words, coming out of their mouths and filling the air. *Bear. Mother. Half-naked. Euthanized. Poor bear. Torn face. Missing fingers.*

I think of the word *unbearable.* My face smiles at the irony. I watch it collide into the other words. Crash and jumble, until the letters dislodge from one another and they're no longer words, just letters. Until they're nonsense, and a big yellow bus suddenly appears in front of me, swallows me up, and takes me away.

• • •

"Tell me what you're thinking," some guy in the guidance office asks me. I haven't bothered to learn his name. Who cares what it is. Who cares what anyone's name is or why we're called what we're called for our whole lives. I can hardly remember my own.

My mom's name was Ruby.

Ruby Falls.

Names are ridiculous.

Dani. Dani Falls. All my life I imagined myself tripping, and all because she refused to give me my father's name. Or maybe, most likely, she didn't know it.

Maybe names do matter. Maybe your future is in your name. Maybe if my father had given me his name things would have been different.

"I wish we could change our names," I tell the guy. "We should be allowed to change our names on a daily basis."

"Why?"

I shrug. Dani. Ruby. Falls. I string them together in my head until none of them make sense.

I stare out the window. The heavy rain of moments ago that had rushed down and sounded like television white noise is stopping. The last heavy drips of silver are being wrung from the clouds and plopping lazily to the ground. Water. Falls.

"Why?"

"What?"

"Why would you like to change your name?"

Is he still talking about names?

"The rain looks silver," I tell him. Rain looks silver. Water looks pink. The water in the pool has turned pink. Drops of water are falling in that pink pool right now. Maybe it's clear again.

The word *pink* reminds me of the nail polish.

And dangling pinkies.

I wonder what made her choose shell-pink. Usually she wore orange or red polish. Flaming-hot colors that made her stand out. All she ever wanted was to stand out. And she did. Her hair, her clothes, her voice. She was loud. There was a pitch in her voice, her laughter, that hurt my ears.

The bell rings. I get up and leave. Mr. So-and-So is still saying something, but his voice trails off as the door closes behind me. I stalk through the office, down the crowded halls, and into a bathroom stall. Another bell rings. I wait until the halls are empty. Until five or six more bells ring and the muffled silence that always follows noise covers me like a blanket. I fall asleep on the toilet. It's the smell of lemons that finally wakes me up.

The custodian is wide-eyed when I come out of the stall. I walk all over her freshly mopped floor.

I feel like a sleeping bear.

I wander around the mostly empty school, realize I've missed the bus and my only choice is to walk home.

But there is no home, my brain reminds me, *and there's no one home*.

I wonder what I should do.

I shrug off the panic creeping around me, look over my shoulder, wonder if the bear made it out of my dreams and followed me here.

I walk until I'm outside the school library, and I tell my brain *Shhhhhhhh, be quiet*, as I reach for the door handle and go inside.

The media specialist looks up from her stack of books and I know instantly that she knows. Those looks are what I felt all day. They're why I hid in the bathroom.

It was one of our students' mom? That's terrible. Which student? Oh, I think I know who she is, the one who comes in here in the mornings. Oh, that's terrible. Just terrible.

The media specialist offers me a sad smile and I want to tell her she doesn't have to be nice, but I walk toward the display of summer reading books instead.

She came to our class and talked about them, the books we had to read over summer. But this one, *The Stranger*, is the one that suddenly comes rushing back to me.

The media specialist stood in front of the class, holding the book in her hand, pitching an absurd story about a strange guy. She tried to make it sound interesting, but I could tell she didn't like it. I could tell she didn't like him, the stranger.

She read the first paragraph to us.

His mother was dead.

I remember.

I wait for something to happen. It seems like something should happen, like the world should shake, like the bear should come crashing through the glass door, shattering the silence, the stillness in the library. The clock ticking high on the wall sounds as if it's being held up to my ear. Each second sounds loud and endless.

I look over at the media specialist, but she quickly looks away.

I stare at the book cover, wondering if the stranger could have known what was going to happen to me before it happened, if he'd been making his way to me even before the bear.

My mother's face fills my mind. Small black dots cloud my vision and I wait for the panic I felt outside to find me.

But it doesn't.

I blink and focus on the cover. He wants me to take him. He wants me to read his story.

I wait again. But nothing happens.

Okay, I say to him, the stranger. I reach for the book and walk over to the checkout counter, to the media specialist, who pretends she wasn't watching me but was. And I set the book down in front of her and we both stare at it.

"We're not checking out books anymore," she says softly. "Too close to the last day of school."

I keep my eyes on the book. "I have to read this," I say. *Because I know how his story starts, but I don't know how it ends.*

She takes the book in her hand. "Do you . . . know what this book is about? There are other books you could—"

I cut her off. "I know what it's about." Because there are no other books. Only this one.

I wait. And I think if she doesn't check it out to me, I'll fight her for it. I'll take it and run.

But after a moment, I hear the soft beep of a scan.

When she holds the book out to me, I don't look at her face. I grab the book and go, clutching it tighter with each step, all the way to Helen's house.

• • •

"Did you talk to Dr. Gary today? At school?" the lady from child services asks. She's waiting for me at Helen's when I get there. I worry she'll know I have *The Stranger* in my backpack and she'll know what it's about and she'll take it away. But she repeats her question and I just nod and try to remember who the hell Dr. Gary is.

"Nice guy, right? He goes to the schools when we need him. They notified us when you showed up today." She shoots an annoyed look at Helen, who is watching television in the other room.

I want to ask her how many others like me she has, and what it's like going around dealing with people's blown-up lives. But I don't. Because that would lead to getting to know her and there's no point in that.

So I say, "He's fine."

"I was going to have you see him once a week, but . . ." She takes some papers out of her briefcase, looks at them, and puts them down. "Well, the thing is . . . your aunt says she'll take custody of you, but you have to . . ."

I stare at her. I don't know what is coming out of her mouth. I try to make sense of her words. But I can't. Because *you said there was no one.*

You have no one but me, Dani!

"An aunt?" I say.

Black dots cloud my vision again and I blink them away.

She nods. "Did you know about her?"

No one but you, that's what you said. That we were on our own! That we only had each other! That I only had you!

I feel like I'm floating.

How many other things did she never tell me? How many other things did she take with her to her grave?

I swallow.

"Maybe, I don't know," I manage to say.

"Your mother's sister. She lives in New Mexico. That's where you'll be moving. And, well, you'll leave in a few days. . . ."

She takes a deep breath, searches my face, waits for me to say something. But I can't.

"Dani?"

An aunt. Somewhere, there had always been someone. Someone other than my mother.

The child services lady looks at me. Her face is concerned, like the media specialist's. But I don't want her to look at me that way. I don't want her comfort or her pity. I don't need it. Or her. I've never needed anyone. Not even my own mother.

"Dani?"

She's waiting for me to fall to pieces.

But my mom was the one who liked falling to

pieces. Who liked people feeling sorry for her. Who groveled for attention. Not me.

Say something, I tell myself. *Say something!*

"Yeah, okay," I tell her.

She looks at me funny. No doubt she came prepared with all the reasons this move would be good. I can tell. I can see the words lined up on her tongue, waiting to be dispatched. I can see her finger on her cell phone for an emergency call to Dr. What's-His-Name. I can see she was ready.

But I'm ready too.

She's saying something now about my school waiving my final exams because of my A average. I don't even have to go back. It will give me time to adjust to all this . . . to prepare for the trip. I focus on her moving lips and nod.

I learned not to get attached to people or places long ago. To simply get up and go without a care about who or what we left behind.

Besides, I don't want to stay with Helen anymore, even if she was nice enough to take me in. In fact, I almost understand why Mom never liked her much. And I don't want to go back to school either. So flying somewhere else is *fine, just fine* with me.

The panic subsides. Everything comes back into focus.

I nod. "Sure. That's totally fine. Will you be taking me to the airport?"

"Uh, yeah. I mean, sure. I can do that." She stares

at me. I wonder if she thinks I'm asking her, if she thinks I need her, when really I just don't know if there's some child services bus that does things like this, takes orphaned kids to airports to fly to faraway places to meet strangers. I try to clarify that I don't need her to take me, but she starts talking before I can.

"You're sure you're okay with all this?"

Again I nod. What say do I have in any of this anyway? This was decided for me; the only solution. I saw it. I understood. What am I supposed to do other than comply?

"I'll be ready," I tell her.

She pats me on the back, a strange little pat, and tells me she'll call with more details. "You sort of amaze me," she says as she stands up.

It's a strange thing to say, but when I look at her, I think she means it. She does look a little amazed. Or scared.

"I'm amazed by bear attacks in backyard pools," I tell her. It's the wrong thing to say, but I don't care.

She winces, then fiddles with her briefcase and takes a deep breath.

"I'll talk to you soon," she says, and leaves.

I sink into the couch. *You're fine*, I tell myself, *you're fine*. If I keep repeating that, I can't hear what the other part of me is saying.

Maybe it'll do me good, going out west. I think of orange sunsets and rust-colored earth.

"So, you're leaving?" Helen asks. She's leaning on the doorframe.

"I guess so." It's not a big deal.

She shrugs. She almost looks sad, or maybe I want her to be, which is odd. She turns and goes back to the kitchen.

An aunt.

Aunt what? I didn't even ask her name.

New Mexico.

I wonder if the dust will fill my nose and cloud my head so I can't think. I wonder if tumbleweeds will roll through my mind and all my memories will get caught up in them and tumble away. I wonder if the bear will leave me alone and stop coming to me in my dreams if I am no longer here.

Because last night, he brought Mom back. She was next to me. But we were on our knees with our hands tied behind our backs. And I knew we were going to be executed.

I just knew it.

But she didn't.

Or she didn't care.

Because she was laughing. I told her to stop. I knew he was near and would hear her and find us. But she wouldn't stop. She just kept getting louder, her high-pitched laughter slicing the air.

Suddenly I realized there was something in her voice that only bears can detect, something that conjures them up and brings them running.

I told her she would get hurt, but she kept laughing. She couldn't hear a thing; she couldn't hear me screaming or crying. He was getting closer.

I could feel the floor shaking as his paws hit the ground running, coming to get us.

And then he was behind us.

And she stopped mid-laugh.

And I waited.

• • •

"Ms. Overton will pick you up at three o'clock," Helen says. We're at my house. School is over, I guess, because June 1 is written on the ticket to New Mexico that somebody bought me and I printed at Helen's. I fold the paper and put it in *The Stranger*, look around my room deciding what to take. I have a couple of band posters, but I only take the one with the guy standing alone, looking away from the camera.

"Ms. Overton?"

"The child services lady." Helen looks at me with her small eyes that I can't read. "You know?"

"Right." I stuff more clothes into my bags.

"Don't worry about the things here. I'll pack them."

Worry? I hadn't thought about any of it. Hadn't even wondered what would be done with it.

"All the furniture was here when we moved in," I tell her. "None of it is ours."

When we lived in apartments, they were always

26

practically empty. Then there were the houses. Small at first. *Isn't this better?* Then bigger. *Look at this. Isn't this better?* She always thought the next place was better.

But no matter where we moved, everything was the same. The rooms, the walls, the schools, even the kids at school. I barely remember the blur of faces that didn't matter after the ones that only sort of did. Like Fanny, who gave me an ice cream magnet and held my hand and told me it meant we were best friends. But that was so long ago; now I wonder if Fanny ever really existed.

Sometimes I forget we moved and sometimes I dream about people and places I'm not sure were real. All the apartments and houses with their rooms and halls had a way of melding into one big, sprawling house with endless halls and mazes. Each new place was another wing added on to this odd house that lived in my memory, and each made things worse somehow, not better.

Helen nods. "Dave and Ken will be here soon, I'm sure. Get it ready to rent again."

"Dave and Ken?"

"The owners." She stares at me. Blinks.

"Right."

I think of Helen walking around our house, going through our things. It makes me uncomfortable.

I push the thought out of my mind.

"I have some space at my house. I can store

everything there until your aunt figures out what to do with it."

I nod. I wish she would stop talking. I wish she hadn't brought up the idea of our stuff at her house. There was hardly any room there, crammed as it was with new and old items. She called the old things vintage and antiques. But they looked mostly like unwanted, damaged trash. I think of how Helen took me in and suddenly wonder if I'm just another unwanted, damaged thing she collected.

"It's kind of strange that your aunt didn't come. I thought she'd attend the funeral."

I'd made myself forget about the funeral. I can't pack fast enough. I want Helen to be quiet, to magically disappear. I've already managed to believe the funeral didn't happen. I'm not even sure I went.

"I can do this by myself. You don't have to help."

She shrugs. "I don't have anything to do." She looks around my room. "You don't have much stuff. When I was your age, my room was so cluttered you could barely walk in it."

I don't want to think of Helen at my age. Or of her room.

I zip up my suitcase, my duffel bag, and my backpack. "That's it," I tell her.

She looks at me. I know she's been generous, but I'm starting to dislike her.

"That's it? What about all that?" She motions to the bottles of lotion on the dresser, the hair products, the clothes that still hang in the closet and the shoes just under them. But it all looks strange, like it belongs to someone else. "Your duffel bag is hardly full."

I shake my head. "No."

She takes a deep breath. "Okay. But you've got some good stuff there," she says, eyeing the dresser. I have a feeling that when I'm gone, she'll take it all for herself.

She sits on my bed. I'm glad I don't have to sleep in it anymore. I turn around and walk out of the room. I walk through the kitchen, keeping my head down, cross the living room.

Don't think of anything. *Play dead!*

I look at the dirty lines between the tiles. How'd they get so dirty? Dave and Buster will think we were pigs.

Those weren't their names. Dave and who? Who did she say? Things are slipping from my mind so easily, and maybe I should be alarmed, but that slips, too, and I forget to care.

I open the front door, squint against the blinding sun. I sit at the entrance and wait.

David and Goliath?

Helen comes out behind me.

"Nothing else?" she asks.

I look down the street for the Avon lady's car. She's not an Avon lady, I know. But she smells like lipstick and thick perfume. In a different way than Mom did.

I reach into my backpack, take out a lipstick I grabbed off the dresser on my way out so Helen couldn't use it.

I write my name on the concrete in front of me. I like how it glides. I like how it looks, how it glistens and melts in the sun. That's what lipstick should be used for.

I study the gravel and dirt left on the end of the tube.

"What are you doing?" Helen says with more surprise than I thought she could ever muster. I shrug and she laughs. Stares at my name. "Okay, well, you going to eat something before you go?" She stands next to me, her hands in her pockets.

I shake my head.

"Come on. It's still a few hours before she gets here."

"I'll wait out here."

"In this heat? Don't be crazy."

"I'll be fine."

"Well then, I guess this is goodbye," she says. "I hope all goes well for you."

"Thanks. You too," I tell her.

She walks toward the house, her shoulders slouching, her hands in her pockets. I don't think she expected any more than that.

• • •

A car eventually appears at the curb. The Avon lady gets out, waves at me. I pick up my bags and climb in her car.

When we arrive at the airport, she parks and leads me inside, I check my luggage. She flashes her child-savior badge and gets a special pass to take me all the way to the gate. She buys me a few things to keep me entertained on the flight—magazines she picks out herself because I just stare at the glossy faces on the covers—and throws in candy and chips for good measure. She wonders if I want anything else.

I shake my head. The airport is cold and I try to understand how I got here, even though I know how. One moment I was staring at the lipstick on the ground and now I'm staring at the lips of a woman on a magazine cover.

We're at the gate and the lady waits with me, gives me an email address and phone number I'll never use. When they call for boarding, she stands up and looks at me earnestly and tells me to contact her if I need anything. Then she gives me a hug and tells me she'll be thinking about me. I'm glad I have all the stuff in my hands so I don't have to hug her back.

She doesn't leave yet, not even when I get in line holding what she bought for me. I look back after I hand the bored-looking man at the terminal my ticket and she's still there. I see myself yelling at her, telling her she shouldn't think about me or the me who came before or the me who will come after. She shouldn't think about any of us and should forget me because I will forget her. But even that would be too much.

She waves. I turn and walk down the tube that leads me to another tube that will shoot me over to New Mexico.

When I settle into my seat, the woman next to me yawns so big and loud I can smell her sour breath. I wonder if she knows how bad it smells. She does it again. Then again.

"Your breath," I tell her finally.

She smiles. "What?"

"Your breath," I whisper. "It's a little sour."

She recoils like I just tried to bite her nose off and gives me a dirty look.

I offer her one of the chocolates the Avon lady bought me.

The woman stares at the chocolate like it's poison and turns away from me. Moments later, I see her cupping her hand to her mouth as she stares out the window, and she doesn't yawn again.

Soon after, the flight attendant takes her place front and center, with her fake seat belt and yellow vest, and I pay attention.

I pay extra-close attention because I know crazy things happen. And this is my first flight.

I check for exits and I feel sorry for the woman

beside me because she doesn't know I would probably trample her to get to the exit in front of our seats.

Or maybe I wouldn't. Maybe I'd stay on the plane while everyone else clamors and screams and yells.

Maybe I'd sit in my seat and close my eyes. Maybe I'd reach for the book in my backpack.

Maybe I'd even smile as the plane plummeted to the ground.

Dani.

Falls.

• • •

Somewhere I get off this plane, somewhere I get on another plane. This time I don't bother to pay attention to the emergency instructions. But the plane stays in the air and safely lands elsewhere. And I'm struck by how miraculous flying really is. How ten-ton metal birds can fly without flapping their wings, how they can defy gravity.

The pilot welcomes us to El Paso, Texas. This is where my aunt will pick me up since it's the closest airport to where she lives.

It's the smallest of airports. Not that I've been to any others. We never traveled, though she always said we would. *We're going to see the world! The world is so big, Dani, and we're not going to stay hidden in the corners of it like roaches. We're not roaches. We're not vermin.*

But somehow, by the end of her slurring and rambling, I was a roach. I was vermin. I was many horrible, terrible things because I didn't believe her. Even though *you have a passport, don't you? You could jump on an airplane right now and go anywhere, couldn't you? Because of me, Dani!*

We never even made it to another state.

I focus on the signs around me to erase her face and mute her words. I go down one small set of escalators and see the baggage claim. I follow the woman with bad breath to an empty carousel. I look around, suddenly wondering how in the world I'll know my aunt.

I see a lot of other people hugging other people. Strangers hugging strangers.

Some back part of my brain whispers, *I bet none of their mothers have gotten mauled by a bear.*

Something beeps and I focus on the shiny metal of the carousel that is now beginning to move. Slowly, pieces of luggage emerge through the rubber fringes of a small opening.

I want to get on the conveyer belt. I want to go through the fringed rubber opening and be in another world. Or maybe someone could just throw me back on the plane so I could fly through the air again, on an airplane flying backward. I want it to taxi into Orlando, gate B45, and spit me out. I want to walk backward through the tunnel that connects the plane to the gate, get my ticket handed back to me by the bored-looking guy. I want the Avon lady to take back her hug, her scrap of paper, and we get back in her car, and she drives me back to a house that was and wasn't mine.

Then I want clocks to spin.

I want nights to rise.

And days to fall.

I want to go back,

back,

back.

I want to be unborn.

But then my red duffel bag catches my eye and I grab it as it passes and pull it off the conveyor belt. Next, the suitcase.

I drag one and roll the other to the outskirts of the crowd and search for someone I don't know.

A woman comes in through the automatic doors holding a piece of cardboard in her hands and I'm sure it's her.

Jeans and a T-shirt.

Short blondish-brown hair, frizzy and wavy.

I watch her go to the large board announcing arrivals and departures. Then she goes to the airline counter. The employee there points to the luggage carousel.

I see the way the woman holds the small cardboard sign in front of her.

Dani Falls.

She searches the sea of faces. She searches over their heads.

And then she sees me.

She walks slowly toward me, her eyes on me the whole time.

"Dani," she says when she's close enough for me to hear. It's not a question. She knows it's me. "I'm Shelly," she adds.

Shelly.

I nod. She looks like Mom, so I'm unable to say anything. I stand there, mute. We stare at each other. Then she leans slightly toward me and I think she's going to hug me, but she grabs my suitcase instead.

"Come on," she says, walking toward the automatic doors again. I follow, dragging my duffel bag behind me.

•　•　•

The mountains are in the distance. El Paso is alive with people, all going on. I watch them as we drive.

Shelly and I don't talk much.

At some point she tells me that it's about an hour to her house. She drives fast, with the windows down, her truck creaking violently with any bump we hit.

We leave the city behind until there is only dust and road and mountains. The sun makes everything orange, like the world has been Photoshopped a bright sepia.

There is a sole car in front of us driving through the desert, headed to nowhere also. I search, waiting for a town to pop up, even as I realize there will only be more dirt, more mountains, more road. The sun is going down. I stare out the window and try to remember how I got here.

The truck jerks suddenly to the left, pulling me out of my foggy thoughts.

Shelly—that's her name, I'm sure—curses as we swerve. There's a thump. She looks in the rearview mirror, regains control of the truck, and shakes her head. Mutters something about jackrabbits as I turn and look out the back window.

I can see it spinning on its back. It's horrible.

So horrible.

The way he's spinning on his back, his little legs and long feet in the air, it looks like he's break-dancing.

Truly horrible.

But I want to laugh. Because in my head, he's a trickster. He's a dance star. I'm thinking of him doing the snake, the robot, and then shooting his rabbit fingers at me while looking at me through black sunglasses.

I let out a weird sound and Shelly glances my way before looking in the rearview mirror again.

I stare out the window and pinch my arms because it takes all I have not to laugh. Some part of my brain tells me I'm messed up.

I worry as we go deeper and deeper into nothingness. Every few miles, I see a house off to the side, so far away from the main road it's hardly noticeable. I fight the dread that it's to one of these houses we are headed. The bear will find me easier out here, out in the open, with nowhere to run.

I put my hand on the door handle and picture myself pulling it, and it's enough, enough just to picture it.

I stay calm.

Soon we come to what looks like a deserted town, the kind I thought existed only in movies. We stop at a four-way stop, then turn right and enter a slightly populated area that I'm not sure could be called a town. Mobile homes seem to be organized in some kind of pattern, but they still look scattered. And vulnerable, like they are huddled together surrounded by nothing but emptiness, like the world forgot about them.

We keep driving and I see a sign for a restaurant that's really a shed with nobody parked in front. We pass a fenced-off area that claims to be the community pool but is abandoned. There's a place that sells secondhand clothes and Popsicles. There's also a Pancho Villa museum with a gift shop that proclaims WE'RE OPEN! but looks very closed. A little farther along, I see a sign for available rooms, but no hotel or motel follows.

And I suddenly know that people don't visit here. People don't vacation here. This is where people are left alone. This is where people, maybe, even come to die. Or never leave and die. Or are dropped off when their mothers die.

I fight my whole body. I fight to keep my heart

steady, my arms from opening the door, my legs from running.

I don't think I could run anyway. I feel like I'm made of rubber. I stare out at the dirt road, the beat-up homes with laundry hanging out to dry. And I wonder which one of these is Shelly's.

Isn't this better? I hear Mom say. Her laughter rings in my ears.

A few minutes after we pass the mobile homes, we are driving up a rocky drive to a large house that stands next to what looks like a barn. A high chain-link fence topped off with barbed wire surrounds both house and barn.

Jesus, I think.

But I'm relieved. At least it's not a mobile home. I can't imagine being trapped in one of those with Shelly for an extended period of time.

Shelly gets out of the truck, unlocks the gates, pushes them open, and gets back in the truck. Slams the door so hard I wince. A light swirl of dust has followed her in and it settles around us.

She roughly shifts into drive again and I realize she does everything roughly. I sneak a look at her, but she's staring ahead.

I wonder if she's violent. I wonder if her words cut and pierce and sting. I wonder if her hand is heavy.

We're jostled over the uneven ground. The crackling of rocks under the tires reminds me of crushing bones.

"Well, this is it," Shelly says, putting the truck into park. She swings herself out the door and I slowly get out, staring at the house. It looks out of place compared to the collection of run-down trailers surrounding us.

"Did you just move here?" I ask.

She shakes her head, hands on her hips. "We've always lived here." I wonder if she is married, but I don't ask.

"I had this built about ten years ago. Used to live in that thing," she says, nodding toward a rusty, broken-down motor home in the barn. "All of us did."

She doesn't offer any more information and starts walking up the wooden steps that lead to the front door.

"Get your stuff," she says. "I'll show you where to put it." She unlocks the door and goes inside.

I follow her directions.

The house is bare. It's furnished but still looks empty. Like all the houses I've lived in.

I suddenly remember the house Mom rented before we found Dave and Buster's.

It was pink. The pinkest damn shade of pink I'd ever seen.

Isn't it great? she said as we pulled into the driveway.

I shrugged. It was pretty horrible, actually.

Four bedrooms, she said, smiling and looking at the house like it was one of the wonders of the world.

Four bedrooms. I couldn't imagine what she wanted with all that space, but it was what she bragged about most whenever we moved to a new place. Nothing less than four bedrooms, like I cared. It was stupid since there were just the two of us. Sometimes three, since Mom's boyfriends always ended up mostly moving in. Even so, we didn't need anything bigger than an apartment. A duplex. A small, two-bedroom house at most.

It would have been easier. Cheaper, too, though Mom never worried about money. And neither did I until I was old enough to realize she couldn't pay rent with the waitressing jobs she'd get here and there and there. But she always paid it. I knew she got money from men somehow. More than that I didn't know. And I didn't want to know.

Why? I mumbled. Without meaning to. I remember the early evening was cast in my favorite kind of rose-colored light. It had been raining and the earth smelled wet and beautiful, too. I wanted to enjoy the moment, but the first shot had been fired.

Why what?

Why . . . do we have to move? Why four bedrooms? I mean, we don't really need four bedrooms. . . .

She shook her head. *You're such an ungrateful little shit, you know that?*

I looked down at the sidewalk, slipped off my flip-flops and felt the wet concrete under my feet. I thought about whether I was a little shit. She always did that, asked me a question I couldn't answer. One that left me silent, taking her crap. I listened to the way she drew a deep breath.

Because, she said, loud, sharp, her voice cutting through the air. *Look at me, damn it!* she yelled. And I did. *We move because there is always better. Always. And I deserve it.* I could've said she didn't deserve anything. But I didn't because I didn't want her to smack me on the side of the head. Not in that perfect light. Not out there on the street with people peeking out their windows, taking us in, already making judgments about Mom's cutoff shorts that showed half her ass and the tank top that was too low. Too tight. Too skimpy.

And four bedrooms because that's what I want. Because I want space, to not feel like the goddamn walls are closing in on me. Is that all right with you? Or would you rather live in some little shithole where you can't even breathe?

What she meant was some little shithole where I was within arm's distance of her everywhere she turned. Where I was the constant that she couldn't escape. Where she couldn't send me to the other side of the house so she could be left alone to do whatever she did with whatever guy it was that week. What she needed, what she wanted was room, space, distance so she didn't feel like *I* was closing in on her. Where *I* wasn't sucking the air out of her nose, her mouth, her lungs. Where *I* wasn't killing her.

Forget it, I said.

She laughed the way you laugh at someone you hate. *You're incredible, you know that?*

No? Yes? What the hell was I supposed to say?

I don't think you really mean that, I said. The words were out and they sounded as sarcastic as they had in my head and it felt good and I was proud of myself. She stared at me.

Fuck you, Dani. You had to ruin this, didn't you? You always have to ruin everything.

I didn't want it to hurt, but it did. *I* had to ruin everything? *Me?*

Fuck you, I thought. *Fuck you right back, Mom.* But I wondered if she was right. If I ruined everything. If I ruined her.

She grabbed some stuff from the car and went inside the house. And I stayed put, feeling the ground under my feet, looking at how the rose-colored evening had turned brown and ugly, and imagining what my life would be like one day without her in it.

Shelly leads me down the hall. I pass blank white walls that reveal nothing, two other rooms that look large and empty except for miscellaneous boxes, a chair or two. None of the rooms look like they belong to anyone.

I wonder if she has a husband or boyfriend who will come home and I'll have to meet him. I look for pictures but there are none.

As if reading my thoughts, Shelly says, "It's just me here, so you don't have to worry about sharing a bathroom or anything like that. And I work a lot, so . . ." She lets the end of her sentence drop off before opening the door to a room at the end of the hall.

I notice it's the one farthest from what seems to be the master bedroom on the opposite side of the hall.

"Here you go," she says. I step past her and into the room, struggling with my suitcase and duffel bag and the backpack strapped on to my back. She doesn't offer to help. She barely looks at me.

The room has only a bed and a dresser. Both look new, and the room is filled with the smell of new furniture. A mirror on the dresser reflects me standing there with my bags. I know it's me, but it doesn't look like me. I'm surprised when I see myself. I'd forgotten what I look like.

"I have the graveyard shift. Starts at three a.m. Make yourself at home. Use the bathroom if you want to shower or whatever. There's stuff in the fridge if you're hungry." She looks at me, then looks away. "I . . . I think I'm going to try to get a couple hours' sleep before I have to go. Any questions?"

Who are you?

Who was she?

Why did she lie?

I keep my lips closed. My voice silent. But Shelly waits for an answer.

She used to do that, too. Just wait.

"I'm good," I say.

Shelly nods and turns to head out. In the doorway she looks back at me.

"You look like her," she says quickly. "Your hair is lighter, but your eyebrows . . . your cheeks . . ." She looks at the floor suddenly, like she can't stand the sight of me. And I wonder if she, too, will hate me. I don't say anything. I stand perfectly still.

"Well, anyway . . ."

I nod. And she turns and goes down the hall, to what I had already guessed was her bedroom, and closes the door. I take my backpack off, let it fall to the floor, and throw myself on the bed. The covers are scratchy.

She's wrong. I look nothing like her. My mom's hair was blond, a full ten shades lighter than my own light brown. And suddenly, the thought that child services got it wrong enters my mind and bubbles with possibility. Maybe this woman isn't my aunt, or maybe my mother wasn't even my mother. Maybe my real mother is somewhere safe and sound, not mauled by a bear, and there is still a chance for me to meet her, to be happy. But just as quickly, the bubbling comes back down to a simmer and stops.

Because if this woman isn't my aunt, then Mom was right. I had no one. No one but her.

I think about showering. I think about eating. Just thinking about both is enough.

I close my eyes and fall into darkness and dream I

am climbing walls and clinging to the beams of a ceiling in a house that is mine but not mine. A house with secret rooms and extra halls that get narrower and narrower. A house with doors made of broken wood, kept closed with broken locks.

Be careful of the bear, I tell no one.

He stalks around below, pretending he doesn't know where I am. But he does. And it's only a matter of time before he looks up and spots me clutching the beams.

I hear the sound of doors opening and closing, of footsteps and car doors slamming. Then the roar of an engine and the crumbling of gravel under rolling tires.

I let the night swallow me up again.

I dream of planes. Of a bear on a plane.

I try to remember the directions for the yellow vest. I look for the exit. I search for the airplane safety card, *The Stranger,* anything that might help, but find nothing. And the woman with sour breath is shoving my chocolates in her mouth while everyone else is reading.

No one is worried. They shouldn't be.

It's me he's coming for, after all.

I pull the yellow vest over my head and close my eyes.

Play dead! I remind myself.

PART
TWO

I wake to a loud brightness and a house silent except for the whir of the ceiling fan blowing hot air over me. I lie there and stare at the fan and let everything sink in. It always takes a moment, especially with my head full of heat, to remember where I am, that this is not just another time we moved.

I'm in New Mexico.

I live here now.

With an aunt named Shelly.

The air conditioner is still broken.

Shelly's Post-it note flashes in my head. That's what she wrote and left on the kitchen counter for me—*The air conditioner is broken*—a few days after I got here. I notice she prefers to leave notes rather than talk to me. Quick scrawls in black marker.

Went to work.

Went to grocery store.

There's food in the fridge. Help yourself to anything.
Be back later.

I sit up and listen for her. My head feels heavy.

It feels like I'm alone, but I get up and check for her anyway. Every room is empty.

So I do those things I always do, things that are automatic and feel normal. Like brush my teeth. Wash my face. Get dressed. Make toast and pour juice.

And then I do things that don't feel normal but somehow have become my normal. Like stare at toast for an hour and at a clock until the numbers don't make sense. And search Shelly's house.

I walk slowly through each room looking for I don't know what. There are three bedrooms, two living rooms, a kitchen, and a basement. All of them large and barely furnished. There are no pictures on the walls.

I tell myself *I'm not like Helen, I'm not interested in taking or collecting anything* as I go in Shelly's closet and look through her clothes. *I just want to know who she is.* But all I see are lots of jeans and T-shirts, which are mostly plain but a few have simple graphics. I think it's strange that she hangs up her T-shirts. I look at each one and realize she must be wearing the one with the faded peace sign on it today. I wonder if she knows I come in here, if she can sense that I've touched her clothes. I wonder if she notices the hangers are not quite spaced how they were. I only sort of worry what she might think if she catches me.

I open her dresser drawers and look through her stuff, which is mostly more clothing. There's a Bible in her nightstand. I open it and look at the words but don't read them. Not really. In her bathroom, I spray her perfume and smell her shampoo.

I also go through drawers in other rooms, in the whole house. Bills and junk mail. I read the fine print. I find pennies and dimes, safety pins. I go down the stairs, into the basement. It's cooler down here. I notice some boxes in one corner, and I think about building a maze or something since I know they're empty, but I don't.

There's nothing. No trace of anything. Each search turns up nothing. But I keep looking even though I don't know what I'm looking for.

When I'm done inside, I go outside because there's nothing else to do. I sit on the porch and wait for time to pass.

I used to tell Mom I was in all kinds of after-school clubs so I'd have an excuse not to go home. I roamed everywhere, looking to be anywhere but there. I spent whole days and nights roaming.

She didn't know a fucking thing about me.

Not a thing.

Nothing.

I stare at the vast brown nothingness of the land.

I wait for darkness.

Some nights I dream of my mother and some nights there is nothing but black and I don't know if I slept

or not. I wake up to the same brightness and whir-
ring fan every morning. Sometimes Shelly is home
and sometimes she's not. Sometimes the heat makes
me feel like I've slept for days, which I don't mind. I
hope whole months have gone by, and then I realize
it wouldn't matter if they did. Every day is the same.

Sometimes Shelly asks me if I want to go to the
grocery store with her. Or into town to Walmart if
I need anything. But I shake my head, tell her I'm
fine, because I don't want to be in the truck with her.
And I know she doesn't really want to go anywhere
with me.

Sometimes I get up and she's coming home from
work and she'll sleep most of the day and then I'll go
to bed early.

Sometimes she tends these little trees and plants
she has growing in buckets in the front yard and she
doesn't know I'm watching her from my window.

Sometimes she sits on the porch and when she
comes inside I go sit on the porch until she goes to her
bedroom.

We say as little to each other as possible.

I can't keep track of the days here. Each one seems
longer than the one before and they form one long rib-
bon of time that keeps unfolding.

I don't know what to do with myself. I just keep
waiting. Waiting for something to happen.

• • •

This morning I wake up to a cool room. The sheets aren't sticking to me. My head doesn't feel like it will burst from the heat. The same silence hangs in the air. When I go to the kitchen, Shelly's at the table, reading the paper, coffee mug in hand. She looks severe.

"Air conditioner is fixed," she mumbles. "Finally."

I don't want to sit down with her, but it seems strange to immediately turn around and go back to my room. I stand in the doorway before deciding to go to the fridge.

Open it, look in, close it, say you're going to take a shower. I see the black marker on the counter and get the urge to write I'm going to take a shower on the table in front of her.

As I close the fridge and head to the hallway, Shelly clears her throat.

"Hold on," she says. "Sit here a moment."

She watches as I come closer and take a seat not quite across from her. We sit there a long time, she mentions some stuff in the newspaper and I nod, say the appropriate *oh*s that we've come to rely on, but today she's getting mad. I can tell; I can sense anger in a person before they can.

"Do you, you know, talk?" she asks finally. She puts the paper down, fills the air with the sound of rustling as she folds and refolds it incorrectly before giving up. "I mean, you've been here, what, three weeks now and you've hardly strung more than two words together at once. Do you actually *speak*?"

Three weeks?

Three weeks?

How can I have been here three weeks?

She's saying something else, but my mind is stuck.

Three weeks? I want to ask her. *Are you sure? Are you absolutely sure?*

A part of me, I think, wants to scream.

Shelly looks at me strangely. But I don't say anything, so she slaps the table and sighs.

"You see? God! What have I gotten myself into?" she says, obviously to herself. But I'm right here. I can hear what she's saying, how she's saying it, the tone of her voice, and she doesn't even care. "I mean, what the *hell* have I gotten myself into?"

My face burns with shame and anger and I suddenly remember this feeling. How I used to feel like this all the time with Mom.

I look at Shelly and wonder just how much like Mom she is.

Somewhere in all those forgotten days, I remember watching the way she moves, the way she's never here, the way she seems to want nothing to do with me.

I want her to know I've noticed.

I almost laugh at myself. I almost laugh out loud, at her. When or what part of me had ever thought she would be different?

I stare at the yellow table and wait. I wait for her to tell me how terrible I am, how ungrateful, how I messed up her life.

I could have not had you, Dani! Did you ever think of that? I could've gotten rid of you.

How many times had I heard that before? How many times had I been reminded that she *had me* and so I was to quietly and without question accept all of her shit?

You shouldn't have! I told her. *Now there are two of us who are miserable.*

I wait for Shelly to say the same things to me.

I could have not brought you here, Dani! You could've stayed wherever you were with some screwy neighbor!

I brace myself. I remind myself words are dull arrows. I close my eyes.

Shelly gets up from the table and stands a long time at the sink. If this were a movie, she'd cry. But she takes a deep breath and says, "I'll make you some toast and eggs." She goes to the fridge, takes out the butter and a carton of eggs, then grabs a pan and puts it on the stove.

I know she wanted to slam that pan. I waited for the loud clatter, but she set it down carefully. I watch as she controls each move, as she turns on the gas stove, sending a blue flame flaring up, and then turns it down. Shelly moves like Ruby Falls and I can't stop looking at her even though I want to. There are a thousand little similarities, even among the differences. The way she rubs her arm. The faces she makes. Her profile. Her wrists. The tilt of her head. It's easy to pretend it's her. If I blur my eyes just a little . . . it *is* her. I make myself focus.

She cracks two little suns into a pan. I hear them sizzle. I watch the way she stands over the stove, lost in her own thoughts.

She scoops the eggs onto a plate, grabs the toast, and sets the plate in front of me.

The eggs look alarmed. *Are you really going to eat us?*

I cut into the white and take a small bite. Shelly sits down, watches me. I stare at the blurry little suns on my plate.

"I'm sorry . . . ," she says. I shake my head. I don't want her apologies. I don't need anyone's apologies. Apologies are a joke, an excuse for people to explode and spew hate and then pretend no one got burned.

"I want to go home," I say. It's a ridiculous thing to say and I don't know why I say it. As soon as the words come out of my mouth, I realize the impossibility. I don't have a home, and home was never a place I wanted to go to anyway.

Shelly's eyes are on me. I can feel them. I stuff the eggs and toast down my throat and then go to my room. I hope she won't come in. I hope she'll just leave me alone.

I choke back the eggs. I sit on the bed and remind myself not to feel.

I think about Helen's stuffy room. I think about the oppressive heat that filled Shelly's house. How it dulled my thoughts. Maybe it had made me delirious.

I look at the chair next to my bed and grab *The Stranger*. My airline ticket falls out from between the pages and I look at the date. June 1.

I open the book to the inside back cover. I mark twenty-one little slashes.

Three weeks.

I try to count backward from there, trying to pin-point the days I left behind.

What day did you die? I try to push the thought away, but my mind keeps going. I hadn't been at school. Neighbors had been home. The night before, I'd gotten home late because it was Friday and I went everywhere but home. So that day must have been a Saturday.

Was it a Saturday?

I mark more slashes, trying to figure out how many days—*weeks?*—passed before I came here.

But I lose track quickly and then there are too many slashes and I don't know which days they stand for, so my hand just keeps making more until the whole back cover is full. And then I look at them and wonder which one, which one exactly, marked the day.

The day the bear came for you.

Shelly's truck roars and I'm alone. I don't know if she has left for a few hours or if she left for work. And I don't care.

I close the book.

. . .

That night, I feel like something is calling me, but I don't know what it is or where I'm supposed to go. I don't even know if it's a voice, but when I close my eyes, I see my mother looking at me softly. And I can't stand it.

Go away, I tell her.

Her face falls, sad, not annoyed, the way she usually looked when we got upset at each other. But I want her to look annoyed. I want her to look at me the way she used to, like she couldn't stand me.

Leave me alone, I tell her. *Go away!*

Why was she calling me anyway? How could she possibly ask anything of me?

She closes her eyes and disappears, and I'm left with just a fading outline of her face, the word *wait* on my tongue.

I wake up, my pillow damp with sweat. I'm afraid to go back to sleep, to see her again, so I don't. I wait for morning.

Maybe it's *The Stranger* calling me.

It's a relief when I see the darkness in the room start to disappear. Except that means it's another day. The ceiling fan comes into view and stays still. The room gets brighter and brighter. I take a deep breath, reach over, and pick up the book from the chair. Black and blue, like a bruise, with a small yellow square around a bright yellow dot and a blurry image of a man. That's him, I suppose. The Stranger.

If I can read this, I'll be fine, I tell myself.

I can handle it.

I suddenly see myself at the kitchen table of one of the places where we lived. Mom's boyfriend's lighter is in my hand. I remember rolling the small metal gear, the tiny grooves hurting after so many tries, and finally seeing the flame flicker to life. I sat there, running my finger back and forth through the yellow because it didn't hurt. It was magic. And I dipped down to the blue flame and it hurt, but I knew I could handle it.

I stole that lighter and did that same trick until my fingers were callused and not even the blue flame hurt.

The book is a blue flame.

It's salt in my wounds.

I open to the first page.

But reading the first few lines makes my brain white-hot and things explode in my head. It leaves me dizzy and dazed. I put the book down, take a deep breath, and try again.

If I get through it, I'll survive. I'll be thick and callused. The pain will calcify and turn to stone. The words will be a hot blue flame that burns my memories and turns them to dark plumes that disappear into the air.

I focus and refocus on the print, but the words keep moving and black dots fill the page. So I stare out the window, at the bright sun, the promise of numbing heat. Maybe *that's* what is calling me.

That's what will burn everything away.

So I go.

• • •

As I walk, I watch the dust rise, fall, coat my shoes with each step. I wonder how it doesn't all just blow away, how the surface of the earth stays intact with wind and people and cars and animals disturbing it every second of every day. But then, I suppose it's always falling back down.

My sneakers go from gray-white to orange to brown. I don't know where I'm going, but I look back every few steps to make sure the house is still in view. *Stay close*, my brain says, but my feet don't obey, because with each step there's a strange sense of power. Walking makes that monstrosity of a house in this vast empty space diminish somehow. It becomes smaller and smaller, until it disappears altogether. And I wonder what other things I can make disappear.

I smile. Like magicians who can make mountains move and volcanoes vanish, *I can make a house disappear.* I laugh. *Dani the Great.*

I keep walking. I recite the alphabet, then count until the numbers get boring; then phrases pop into my head.

And miles to go before I sleep!

Ninety-nine bottles of beer!

Need an attorney? Call Biddle and Biddle at 1-800-something-something-something . . .

I look up and see a gas station appear in the distance.

I can make gas stations appear. I walk toward it, stomping my feet harder into the earth just to make the dirt swirl high, higher, higher, because I like the way each dust cloud hypnotizes me, the way my legs get coated with a layer of orange that keeps building on with each kick. I like the way it makes me think of *dust, only dust. Dust is all that matters!*

There's a door in front of me. I open it and walk into an even thicker blanket of heat.

A guy is sitting behind the counter, and he glances over at me as I come inside. A newspaper is spread out in front of him and a television is on. The face of a woman with sleek black hair fills the screen. I know her face, this scene. I've seen it before, but I can't make sense of it.

The guy catches my eye. He looks sleepy. He looks like a dream. The woman on the screen starts dancing to some kind of old music and I look at her, but she's looking at the man she's dancing with, another familiar face. I wonder where I know them from. The guy watches me before turning his attention back to the television. I turn down the first aisle.

The aisle is full of car supplies. Motor oil and tree-shaped air fresheners. Windshield wipers and wiper fluid. Somehow this leads to toothpaste and dental floss. Deodorant. Then maps. Everything is in packages that are crumpled at the corners and discolored, as if they've been here forever. Forever.

My mind takes out the *or.*

Fever.

You give me fever. Fever! I see her face. I hear her voice, the way she would sing that stupid song in the kitchen and dance. Out of nowhere. I focus on the items on the shelves.

I walk slowly past them, to the end of the aisle, and then turn down the next aisle as the music coming from the television seems to get both louder and softer.

I take inventory of all the common and odd objects. I see the *Mad* guy smile at me with his goofy grin, black-and-white crosswords make my eyes feel out of focus, and women's lusty eyes peek out at me from the covers of pornographic magazines in sealed packages.

Fever!

I close my eyes for a minute, but that makes me so dizzy, I open them again.

The guy at the counter glances up as I make my way to the third aisle. This one starts with soups: canned soups and soups in envelopes and ramen noodles, but the letters of the alphabet soup make me dizzy again and the pictures of noodles and chicken and vegetables make me feel sick.

I move on to the candy. Chocolate bars and gum and candy so sour it might make your head explode like the cartoon guy on the package. *Or you can walk in the sun; that'll make your head explode, too,* I tell him. At the end of the shelves stands a tin bucket filled with tiny square packets of beautiful gum.

Ten cents!

Neon pink, red and green, purple and yellow and white. I sink my hand into the bucket and imagine diving into a pool full of these little packets, being engulfed by the pretty colored squares. I can hear the clicking of shells as I sink, the smell of candy dye and gum and mint.

It's beautiful.

I pull my hand out, feeling but not dislodging the packets stuck between my fingers. I look at the shelves, like I'm trying to decide. And as I watch the guy stare at the TV screen, I carefully put my hand in my pocket, tucking several pieces of gum there.

I walk on, toward the drinks. Beer. Water. Soda in every color.

But none of it is as beautiful as that gum. And I'm anxious to leave, to feel the crunch of it in my mouth, the sweetness of it flow onto my tongue.

I make myself walk slowly. I make myself look bored. And then I walk to the front, past the guy at the register. My head throbs and my eyes won't focus, but I continue outside, to the bright sun, the orange dust, the only things that make sense.

The air is still hot, but cooler than inside the store, and I can smell it, heat and dust and dust and burning. Each breath I take brings it into my lungs.

I feel in my pocket for the tightly wrapped gum. I take a piece out and admire its bright, bright pink before opening it and popping a single square into my mouth. It tastes just like I knew it would, like Pepto-Bismol.

She'd give me Pepto-Bismol when I had a stomachache. I hated it. It made me gag, but she'd make me take it even as I choked on the thick liquid. One time I spit it out all over the floor and the neon pink splashed on our feet and across the white tile like some kind of art piece. I remember how pretty it looked right before she whacked me so hard on the side of my head, I thought my head had fallen off. Hard enough that a hot, electric sensation zapped through my neck. She was a blur then, her hand over her mouth, horrified. I cried and the way she stared at me, frozen like that, I thought maybe I was headless. Or maybe pink rivers were flowing from my eyes.

"I'm sorry," she said. "I'm sorry," she kept saying as she refilled the spoon, her hands shaking. "Just take it, *please, please!*" I couldn't stand the pain in my stomach. I didn't want to be swiped on the side of my head again. I didn't want her hands to keep shaking the way they were shaking, but I wouldn't open my mouth.

I knew it would make her angry. But I didn't care.

She yelled and told me how I made her do it, so I shut my lips tighter. But then she held me somehow so my nose was plugged and then she shoved that spoon into my mouth and made it clatter against my teeth so that I thought they might break. I gagged, but could do nothing but swallow the pink slime, and that made me get angrier and cry harder, while she cursed and walked away and slammed the door to her room.

I went to my own room, my feet sticky with pink. And I crawled into bed and closed my eyes and wished the world would disappear. Only when I was too tired to cry anymore, when I was somewhere dark and beautiful, did I feel the warm wetness of a towel wiping my feet. And then the warmth of her hands as she kneeled at my bed and held my hands. But I was so far into the dark and beautiful, I couldn't open my eyes. I felt her tears on my hands. Her lips on my forehead. Her words slipping into my ears, into my dreams. She was sorry. And she was praying.

And I loved her so much in that moment. Even though there was a part of me where the hate was growing.

I pop the second and third and fourth squares of gum in my mouth. Each time I crunch through one, I see an explosion of pink behind my eyelids, and the thick liquid gushes into my mouth. I gag. I can feel sweat all over me, and how the dirt sticks to my skin when I fall and stare up at the impossibly bright sky.

It's so white, so hot, that I can't hear anything except what's inside my head. It feels like I'm in an airplane, and suddenly I wonder if I am. If the world is going in reverse. And I wonder if this is what it feels like to be unborn.

My ears plug up and maybe my blood is boiling. Maybe this is the sound of a rolling boil I hear. I imagine gurgling red bubbles in my head,

There are black dots everywhere I look. The harder I look, the larger the black dots become, until they blot out the sun. Until they swallow me up and I can't remember where I am or how old I am or what is now.

There's a deep grumble and I remember the bear.

Leave me alone. But he's grabbing my arm, and soon he'll be biting my pinkies.

I should scream; I should run.

Are you okay? Are you okay?

My eyes snap open and the sun blinds me again. The world is an asteroid.

A shock of something cold brushes against my arm and then I'm being pulled backward. I should be scared, but it feels good. It feels good to be limp, to be dragged, to not care. Maybe he'll bury me.

But moments later, I'm sitting against something solid. And there's water wetting my lips.

I look over. Someone is holding a water bottle to my lips, but the harder I try to focus, the less I can see. I catch a glimpse of his mouth moving, lips glistening in the sun. I look up, to his eyes, try to take his face in all at once instead of bit by bit.

It's the guy from the gas station. He's saying something I don't understand. I feel a cold wetness against the back of my neck, so cold it burns my skin and sends jolts through my body.

"Are you okay?" The words finally take meaning through the layers of thick heat. "Here, drink some more," he says, putting the bottle of water in my hand. The coldness sends a fresh set of shocks through my body, but I hold the bottle and drink from it.

"You fainted," he says.

I stare at the gas pumps, red and gray and chipped with white, and they look pretty somehow. I try to tell him that, but my mouth is still thick with the taste of pink and chalk.

I drink more water. Little droplets fall from my chin.

"Better?" he asks. My head feels heavy and hurts, but I can see clearly. The gas pumps seem to be getting crisper, clearer, so I nod. Just nodding makes the world spin, and the pain in my head takes sharp turns.

"Hold on, wait here," he says.

I close my eyes, but that makes everything worse, so I open them and somehow he's back without ever leaving. I think he's Flash Gordon, and I start to mumble that to him, but he shushes me and helps me walk to a truck that has suddenly appeared in the middle of the desert.

We walk toward it.

For days we walk.

I try to tell him he's the slowest Flash Gordon ever, but I just laugh instead and wonder where the gas pumps went.

Then he is shoving books and DVDs off the seat

and to the floor and we are inside the truck. I am sitting on torn brown leather, so hot it burns my legs, and I am holding the bottled water to my forehead and I am taking deep breaths. He gets in and we drive away and I only sort of care or wonder where we're going.

I watch the side mirror, the gas station getting smaller and smaller, the pumps reappearing in miniature, and all of it becoming a portrait as a film of orange dust floats up in front of it.

I close my eyes, lean my head on the window, then lift it again when it bangs against the glass as we drive.

We come to a trailer.

"I'm fine," I tell him, surprised that my voice works. The words are thick and slow, but they come out. And I don't want to get out of the truck. I stare at my legs and shoes, layered with dirt. I stare at a book under my feet. Something about films.

"My grandmother's home. She'll make you feel better."

He calls for someone and I think my ears don't work, but then I realize he's speaking another language, Spanish.

¡En español!

The voice of my Spanish I teacher floats into my mind, the sharp clap of her hands. *¿Cómo estás, Dani?* as I walked into her classroom.

Mal, Señora Lopez. Muy mal.

A woman appears at the door, her voice calm as she

replies to the guy and holds the door open. We climb the few wooden steps leading to the entrance and I look at her as we pass. Her hair is long and mostly gray, peppered with strands of black. A brown shawl covers her shoulders, and jewelry hangs from her neck and wrists.

The inside is dim. The guy sits me on the couch, presses the water into my hands. Words I don't understand are exchanged between the two of them, pretty words that sound like they're rolling down from the mountains, echoing around us.

"¿Qué pasó?"

"Se desmayo. Le di agua pero sigue igual."

"Mucho sol."

The woman leans down and looks at me with watery gray eyes, the whites splotched with dark spots and tiny red veins. "El sol es el *diablo*," she whispers. She looks familiar somehow. I think I met her in a dream once.

Her trinkets jingle against each other like wind chimes.

She turns and goes to the kitchen. The guy pulls up a chair and sits across from me.

"Who are you?" I ask him finally. My mouth feels solid again, not like softened wax the way it did earlier, and I think about that for a moment. Was I melting in the desert? Becoming a puddle?

"I'm Paulo. You fainted in front of the gas station

my grandmother owns." He nods toward the old woman, who is now filling a kettle with water. "I work there."

He searches my face for some kind of recognition and I remember flashes of him watching me as I went up and down the aisles, as the woman danced on the TV screen.

"Yeah," I say, nodding. "I remember."

"What's your name?" He leans closer and I catch a glimpse of his eyes. A brighter gray than his grandmother's. Behind him, something dark, a shadow that becomes a figure, moves into view.

It's the bear, standing on his hind legs. He fills up the room and blocks the light from the window, making the whole place darker. I see the way he looks at me and sways to music I can't hear. I close my eyes, try to stop the swaying feeling, try to keep the sudden gurgle in my stomach from erupting.

"Hold on," Paulo says. He moves quickly, comes back with a small kitchen bucket as water shoots from my mouth and through my nose. I cough and choke on it. Pink water.

The kettle whistles.

"Jesus," Paulo says, handing me a paper towel. I take it and wipe my mouth, my nose.

"I'm fine," I tell him. "Really." I sit there with the bucket in my hands until he takes it away.

"You fainted," he says. "You're dehydrated. How long were you walking?"

I shrug. The day feels endless, but the flashes of me walking out there seem only like seconds now.

Paulo sits back down as his grandmother comes over with a cup in her hand.

"Niña," she says as she hands me the cup. "Toma." Her movements are slow and deliberate. She looks like she's never tripped in her life. I hold the cup in my hand.

"Go ahead," Paulo says. "It's just tea, but it'll help."

They watch me. I close my eyes, bring the cup to my nose, and let the minty steam rise to my face. I take a deep breath. Mint and lemon and honey and earth and warmth fill my nose.

"Drink it," Paulo's grandmother says. "Slow." Her face is etched with cracks. Her hair and clothes flow down around her. Her fingers are adorned with glittering rocks. She reminds me of a mountain.

I take a sip and look around the mobile home searching for the bear, but he's gone.

"Todo," she says, pointing to the tea. "But slow." She walks across the room and sits at a table near a small window, humming to herself.

There are little jars of paint and brushes on the table. Next to the table, propped against the wall, are wooden crosses. Some of the crosses are brightly painted and dotted with glittering beads. Others seem to be waiting their turn. Paulo's grandmother lifts a plain cross and begins painting it. She looks over at me as she works.

I feel like she knows the bear and that makes me uneasy.

"Paulo will take you home," she says, turning her attention back to her work.

"Thank you," I say to her, lifting the teacup.

She nods slowly and keeps painting.

• • •

The sun is going down when Paulo and I step outside the trailer. The smell of the tea is still in my nose, but now it mixes with the hot, dry air of the desert.

Somehow we arrive at Shelly's. It's only when we're in front of the house that I remember Paulo asking where I lived. I wonder what I answered.

I stare at him, see his lips move, and know he's just asked me a question. His words make their way to my brain. "When did you get here?"

Shelly's voice rings in my ears. *Three weeks.*

I suddenly remember the plane.

I remember the sun and the steps to a house far away that was and wasn't mine.

I stare at Shelly's place. Was it still three weeks ago, or has more time passed? "I don't know," I say, because I'm not sure. A feeling of panic washes over me. I have arrived at a time warp, where time moves slower, where days feel like light-years and then get lost.

I swallow the panic, reach for the door handle, and pull.

Get out.

Walk.

The rocks roll under my shoes. Perpetual pebbles to trip over.

"Hey," Paulo calls. "Hey!"

I turn and he's still there.

"What's your name?"

Only one name flashes through my mind. It shoots out of my mouth before I can stop it. "Ruby," I call back.

He tilts his head to the side. "Ruby," he says. "All right, Ruby. I'll see you around, then." I watch him drive away.

I don't know why I wonder if he will whisper it later, in the darkness. If he will remember me sprawled out in the desert and think, *Ruby.*

Ruby.

Ruby.

I wonder if I can whisper it later in a dark bathroom, say her name into the mirror, and wait for her to appear.

• • •

I walk slowly up to the front door. Shelly's truck is here. I take a deep breath and open the door.

When I walk in, she looks up from the book she's reading and stares at me as I cross to the kitchen.

"Are you okay?" she asks. The words pound in my head. "Dani? What the hell happened to you?" She's up from the couch and coming over to me quickly and I try to get past her but she grabs my chin to study my face. "Let me see what's the matter with you."

What's the matter with you? You were always asking me that. I was never right. I was never the way you wanted me to be. I didn't know how you wanted me to be. Maybe you wanted me to be like you, but I wasn't. I didn't want to be. So you always thought something was wrong with me.

I called for you once, before I knew better; I called and you didn't come. So I called louder, and louder, until I was screaming. Until my head pounded.

What's the matter with you! *you said, gripping my shoulders and shaking me.*

What's the matter with you! *you said as some guy stared at us from the doorway and laughed.* Are you trying to kill me? Goddamn it, what the hell is the matter with you!

And then you pushed me, so hard I can still feel your hands on my chest.

Maybe it's you, squeezing my heart?
You sent me tripping,
and falling
backward onto some toys.

You stay in here! *you yelled.* You stay the hell in here until you stop that shit!

But I just wanted to see if you'd come. I just wondered what it would take to make you come running.

"Dani, let me see."

"Stop!" I tell Shelly, pulling my chin out of her hands and pushing her away hard. She stumbles backward and I see the look on her face before she quickly recovers.

"Dani . . . ," she says.

"I'm . . ." *sorry. I don't know why I did that. I'm not like that! I've never done that.* "It's just . . . the heat," I tell her as I look down at the floor. She stands there and I do too.

My eyes fill with tears and I hate myself. *Feel nothing!* I tell myself. *Feel nothing!* But I feel something and I think it's shame, knowing what she must be thinking of me.

I mumble something about seeing her in the morning and go to my room.

There are too many memories. Coming too fast.

I close my eyes, but when I do, I see Mom and the way she used to look at me. And then I see Shelly and the way she just looked at me.

And I hear the rumble of the bear, reminding me he hasn't forgotten about me.

• • •

I think he'll say something when he sees me, but he doesn't. Instead, Paulo watches me as I walk through the store. I know he sees me grab the orange soda, take gulps of it, and put it back in the cooler. I know he sees me, and still he doesn't say anything.

He watches me pick through the gum, taking only the pink ones and shoving pack after pack in my pockets.

I look over at him. His eyes meet mine.

He watches me flip through the *Guns & Ammo* magazine on the rack. He watches me read the nutritional information on a bag of chips. He watches me take the calendar off the wall and carry it with me when I leave.

He doesn't stop me. I wonder if I dreamed the other day.

I look at the sky and blink at the sun, that hot and terrible ball of fire that burns and makes the burn of memories easier. And I walk.

Bits and pieces of her float into my mind and I let them.

I tell myself to put one foot in front of the other. I tell myself to keep going.

She had men over all the time. She would choose them over me. It was always *Go to your room!* It was always *Don't come downstairs!*

At night, the sound of their laughter would come up to my window. They'd be in the pool. She looked like a ghost in that pool, laughing as one of them kissed her neck. As she climbed on top of them. Forgetting I was there. Always forgetting I was there.

I remember the first paragraph of *The Stranger.*

> Maman died today. Or yesterday maybe,
> I don't know. I got a telegram from the home:
> "Mother deceased. Funeral tomorrow. Faithfully
> yours." That doesn't mean anything. Maybe it
> was yesterday.

I think of how Meursault tells his story, just an account of an event. No feelings, no emotions.

I don't know what day her funeral was. But I should, right? Daughters should know the days their mothers died, the day they were buried. Maybe I should have saved the memorial program.

The funeral parlor was dim. I think it was dim. People were black spots and dots on the side. But she was front and center. Just like always. And Patsy Cline was singing. Patsy was there.

Mom's color was off. Neither her usual brown tangerine nor the pale gray I had feared and almost expected. She was a strange, murky color.

She wore a red top, red as her name. And a gold sequined skirt.

I hated that top and that skirt. I don't know who picked them out. But what did it matter? I couldn't even remember how I got there.

A few bikers showed up with their old ladies. That's

what they call the women who ride with their arms clasped around a man's waist, holding on to him for dear life. I think my mom wanted to be an old lady, but I never understood why. All of them, the bikers, the old ladies, all of them always wore black.

What were they constantly mourning?

Last summer, we went to bike week. She made me go because the twentysomething son of one of her boyfriends' was going. She and I rode on the back of their bikes all the way to Daytona Beach.

I watched her as we rode, the roar of rumbling thunder in my ears. That time she wasn't clutching her boyfriend. Maybe that was why I noticed. She had her hands on her thighs, like she didn't need anyone. She didn't wear a helmet because it was too practical. Or maybe she didn't wear a helmet because she wasn't afraid to die. Maybe she even wanted to.

The thought had never occurred to me. What *did* she want? I would never know.

I remember the way her hair whipped back like a yellow flag flapping behind her. She had her eyes closed and a strange smile on her lips. She lifted her face to the sky; the sun hugged every curve of it. Slowly, she raised her arms over her head and let the wind wash over her. If you didn't know her, you'd think she was praising God. You'd think she was washing herself of sin.

She glowed. And I was awed. This wasn't my

mother. Wasn't the sin-loving, drinking, tired-looking woman I knew. This was someone else.

This woman was the wind. She was capable of traveling at a hundred miles an hour, leaving everyone and everything behind. She could travel over hot waters, gaining strength, spinning into hurricanes. Blowing over the earth, roaring through foreign lands, whispering into meadows.

She looked over at me, but she couldn't see my eyes through the dark helmet I wore. I was Darth Vader.

The lines came back to her face, marionette lines around her frown. She lost all her strength. She clutched her boyfriend and turned her face away from me, pressed it against the hot leather of his jacket.

That was my mother.

I was her villain.

Why had I looked at her in that coffin? Why hadn't I told someone to screw the lid on and not take it off, like Meursault had? Smooth wood. So much better than covered-up sutures and the clothes she wore to pick up men.

Why had I gone to the funeral? I can't remember who was there other than the bikers. Maybe an elderly lady over to my right. Who would that have been? I think I remember a cotton-candy puff of white hair somewhere there.

They were all strangers. That's why I don't remember them. That's why I can't recall their faces. They were neighbors who hated her. Who hated me. Who thought, probably, I would turn out just like her.

It didn't matter. It was her moment. There were lights shining down on her. When I stood in front of her and looked down, I focused on a single sequin until it was a blurry sun. I stared and stared until I sat down.

I remember someone with a Bible. And I remember Patsy singing about falling to pieces, just before someone wondered if we'd accepted Jesus into our hearts.

Someone else shoved cookies shaped like flowers into my hand, along with a cup of coffee.

I ate and drank.

And then I was in Helen's house, where I threw up, but I don't remember cleaning the mess up. The vomit was bitter. I must have retched in a corner, or a vase, or a closet. Somewhere dark. Only now do I remember and feel bad that my vomit might still be there.

Meursault walks behind his mother's hearse with an old man he doesn't know but who is his mother's friend. Pérez. That's the old man's name. He is too old to walk the distance, but he does.

It's a gesture of love. A last great gesture.

And in the end, he faints struggling to keep up.

It's the image of Pérez that makes me roam the desert, that ridiculous old man performing a great gesture of love for a woman who must have been awful since her son feels no grief for her. But I picture Pérez's big wide eyes, the tiny red and black veins that erupt on the yellow where there should be whites. I picture the sweat on his face. I picture him dabbing a hand-kerchief to his forehead. I picture him panting.

Delirious with heat and struggle and grief. For a horrible woman.

It's the old man who kills me. It's the old man, walking until he passes out, who I understand. Walking until the world goes black.

• • •

I wake up and I don't know if it's dusk or dawn. I wait and the room gets brighter. It's another day.

I pick up *The Stranger.* I try to start each morning this way, reading about Meursault. I had expected the novel to revolve around his mother and what a hor-rible woman she was that he couldn't even grieve her.

But it's about Meursault and how he walks through the world unaffected.

I like the idea of that. I like the idea of nothing mattering, not deeply. Especially not memories. Mem-ories can be just events if we take the emotion away.

It's because of Meursault that I am able to look up a central Florida news website after dinner one night, while Shelly gets ready for work. It's because of Meur-sault I can find the story about the bear. About Mom. And I finally figure out what day she died. It's just a day. A day, in so many ways, like any other.

I wonder if I can tell Shelly. We don't talk about the shove I gave her. We don't talk about how or why we avoid each other. We don't talk about time or how the sun keeps rising and setting. But I wonder what she would say if I told her.

The day Mom died was May 22.

I mark it on the calendar I stole, forgot about, then remembered.

I write it in black marker.

Mom died today.

And then I start slashing through all the days that came after.

"It's been forty-one days," I tell Shelly when she comes into the kitchen and pours coffee into a thermos. She thinks I can't even speak, so I wonder what she will say to this.

She screws the lid on to the thermos. "I know," she says softly. And I wonder if she really does.

"There was a time long ago when she took me to the zoo," I tell Shelly. Because they are just words. And it is just a fact.

I turn around and she's looking at me. She seems a little shaken, but she keeps her gaze steady, searching for something in me, asking me something without asking.

Do you want to do this? Now?

At the zoo, Mom didn't wear a bra. I don't know

why I remember this detail. Probably because most of the day, I was distracted by my mother's breasts making an appearance from the sides of her loose black tank top. I was distracted by the looks she got. Each time I wanted to pay attention to the animals, all I could do was look and see if either breast had escaped.

What? she asked. It was always defensive or exasperated, the way she said *What?*

Nothing, I said. She studied my face the way she always did, seeing something, confirming something about me. She didn't believe me.

Shelly has one hand on the counter, and something about it looks like she's leaning on it for support.

Do you want to do this? Now?

No. No, I don't. "Another double shift?" I ask, looking at her thermos.

If I were Meursault, I would tell Shelly everything about our lives right now. Just ramble with no emotion. A part of her is waiting for me to do just that, I think.

"Yeah," she says. She takes a deep breath. "I should be home around six in the morning."

"Cool."

"But I can find someone to cover if you . . . if . . ." *You want to do this. Do this now.*

"No," I tell her quickly. "I'm just . . . I was just thinking how I've been here for—"

"Dani . . ."

"Really, go. I'm . . . I just remembered is all." *And I wanted to see if I could say it out loud. I wanted to see if I could still speak.* "I'll see you in the morning," I tell her, turning back to the computer screen.

Please go, please go.

"In the morning, then," she says. The slow scrape of the keys and the thermos across the counter fills the air.

I nod and busy myself at the computer. I type in the name of the zoo again.

"I'll lock the gate," she calls out before closing the front door.

I nod, even though I know she's already gone.

I stare at the computer screen, at the zoo website, the smiling faces of families having fun with animals. Families like that don't exist. Not really. Not here, or at the zoo.

This isn't enough, Dani? she asked. She shook her head and wiped a hand, greasy and salty from popcorn, on her tight black jeans. *It's not enough I take the day off to bring you here, to smell animal shit all day? You're still like this?* She shook her head again and I could see her anger growing. *Nothing is enough for you. I can never do enough.*

I wouldn't feel sorry for her. I was tired of her poor-me routine. Besides, I already knew what a liar she could be. She hadn't taken the day off. She'd been fired. It was on the tip of my tongue to tell her I knew. But I didn't.

I'm sorry, I said, even though I didn't mean it. I could lie too. *I'll become a better liar than her*, I thought. And I softened my face and smiled as genuinely as I could. She stopped. It almost felt like a game. Could I trick her? She took a deep breath and nodded.

Fine, she said, but she shook her head like she was just too tired to fight with me.

I was too much, I guess. I was too much for her. She was always tired of me, always shoving me away. I was always bothering her. I took up seconds. I took up minutes and hours and years. I was greedy.

I was a constant that was like a life sentence.

Without thinking, I slipped my hand into hers and felt her cringe. What I want to ask her was why she had me. Why, if she hated me so much, did she bother to have me?

"Stop being so needy," she said.

I let go.

We'd been to the giraffes and fed crackers into their ugly mouths. Then we passed the monkeys climbing trees and ropes. And we saw the bear.

He stood behind a large sheet of glass and stared at her as if he'd been waiting for her. Other visitors came up, tapped on the glass, trying to get his attention.

But it was Mom he noticed.

And she stared at him, like she was trying to place where she knew him from.

That floor-to-ceiling sheet of glass, whose whole job was to reveal everything and hide nothing, was all that stood between him and us. No steel bars, no cage, just glass. The bear stared at us.

"He scares me," I told her.

This time she reached for my hand. And she held it so hard and so tight, I thought she was angry at me again. I thought she would tell me how ridiculous I was. How many other kids loved the zoo and all I could do was complain about being afraid of the animals.

But she didn't say any of those things. Instead she said, "Me too." She started dragging me away. But the bear followed. He followed until the glass ended. And when I looked back, he stood at the edge watching us go, pawing at the air, at the nothingness between us.

Here's what I didn't tell you, Mom. As you stared at him, I wondered, what if he broke through the glass? What if he reached out with one giant paw, grabbed me, and pulled me in? What if he throttled me until my teeth knocked into each other and shattered? What if he clawed at me, mauled me? I pictured that because I wondered what you would do.

I would cry out for you. Even though I wouldn't want to, I knew I would. I would scream for you.

And then I imagined myself on the ground, dead. The bear satisfied. I imagined you weeping over me. A thousand times I'd pictured this. When we'd drive home from the store and I pictured an accident with one fatality, an airplane falling from the sky, crashing and burning into just my room somehow, a hidden disease ravaging my body. I pictured all these things, and each time, I imagined you weeping over me. You *weeping over* me. *I wasn't supposed to weep over you. Because you weren't supposed to ever leave.*

But then you let go of my hand again and I remembered, you could hardly stand to hold it. So I couldn't quite picture you weeping anymore.

But I couldn't quite picture you just walking away either. Leaving me alone with the bear.

So I wonder, Mom, what did I mean to you?

When I saw that bear pawing at the air, staring after her, I felt something. Maybe I knew even then that someday he would come for her.

And he'd get her.

And I'd be out here in the desert by myself, feeling even lonelier, even more left-behind, than I ever had before.

I click on the website. I search for the bear we saw that day. But the zoo no longer has a bear exhibit and I don't find any mention of him anywhere on the site. He didn't have a name. He wasn't a favorite. He wasn't transferred to another zoo. He didn't die. He didn't have a family. It's as if he never existed. Except he did.

I think he must have escaped.

I think he must have cut a large circle in that glass and put it back. He must have smoothed it over with his magic paw, binding the glass together again so nobody would ever know how he left.

The zookeepers must have walked into that empty

glass area the next day and scratched their heads. He would have been long gone by then. He would have been traveling down secret pathways, hiding, biding, settling into the woods behind the house we would someday rent.

He would have been watching.

And waiting.

He saw me through the sliding glass door that day. I'm sure he did. Watching, seeing if I would come out.

But I didn't. I was the one who walked away and left her out there alone, beyond the glass. Trapped.

And I was deaf to her screams.

Stop! I tell myself.

There is nothing on the website about any past exhibits at all. Maybe because nobody ever looks these things up.

Or maybe because one day they lost a bear.

In the morning, I hear Shelly come in. I hear her boots scraping the floor as she walks down the hall. She opens my bedroom door and I pretend to be asleep. She closes it.

• • •

I pass by Paulo's trailer and listen to the music coming from the open windows. I walk because of the sun. Because of how it burns my mind. I walk because telling yourself to be numb is not enough. Because the more I want to be numb, the more time passes, the more slashes I make, the harder it becomes.

A woman sings. Her voice is like jagged metal, sharp and cutting around the edges. She whispers warnings, or maybe threats. Maybe longing. I sit on the ground under one of the windows and listen.

I put my head on my knees, shielding my face from the hot sun, and close my eyes, trying to understand the words.

The woman keeps speaking. Softer, barely a paper whisper. She knows all the secrets in the world. But then it stops abruptly, the woman's voice coming to a sudden, angry silence.

I open my eyes and look up to see Paulo's grandmother looming above me, leaning her head out the open window, her hair falling like a canopy around her.

I hurry to my feet.

"Hi," I say.

She nods. "Paulo is not here," she says. "You like the music?"

I nod.

"You know what it means?" she asks.

She waits for an answer, but I don't say anything. "You know," she tells me. "You know."

I stare at her.

I know her from my dreams. I remember her coming down through the ceiling and out from under my bed. I think she was there when the bear was pounding the earth, coming for us. She stares at me, her face stern.

"Dolor," she says. The word is a soft puff that escapes her lips like smoke. She closes her eyes. "Dolor," she whispers again, clutching her heart. Her face takes on a look of devotion and pain. "Dolor."

Something startles in my heart. I feel it being squeezed. I watch her hand, dark and wrinkled with slightly deformed fingers, squeeze at her chest, her rings catching and reflecting the sun. Each time, I feel my own heart being squeezed, the blood pumping faster and forcefully.

"Dolor," she says. *"Dolor."*

I stumble backward, clutching my chest, trying to calm my heart back into submission.

I want to tell her to stop. But I can't. Each squeeze leaves me breathless. I turn and walk away, fast, faster, until I'm running.

I run away from her squeezing of my stone heart. Pumping life into it. Making it feel real again.

• • •

Up ahead, I think I see a girl and a guy about my age walking. They shove each other playfully and I wonder if they're desert ghosts because I haven't seen anyone else outside since I got here. The boy says something and the girl smacks his arm and shoves him harder. He laughs and I remember how my mother's laughter conjured the bear and I want to warn them. But they dissipate into the orange dust before I can reach them or open my mouth.

I feel a phantom squeeze my chest, the clench of an invisible fist. My head pounds and I know I've been walking for too long, but I stomp my feet harder against the ground, making them and my legs ache. I look at the black armband tied tight around my arm and make a fist with my hand, which hardly feels like my own anymore. I concentrate on how the sun is burning my skin. I look up at it, purposely blinding myself, making myself dizzy.

I'm tired. I should go home and find out about Meursault, because there's something he's trying to tell me. I almost feel like I know what it is, but I keep walking because it's all I can do and I forget Meursault and part of my brain pictures me lying on the ground. My head feels numb and I stare at the orange earth and I wonder why my arm feels like deadweight and then remember.

I got the idea to wear an armband from the book, but I don't know why I did it.

I wanted to forget about her, but I couldn't stop myself from remembering. Maybe remembering was the only way to forget.

She would take me to the beach. In the middle of the day, at the hottest hour. I didn't like it much. I sat next to her and built sand castles while she rubbed oil on herself and lay on a towel.

She'd bring beer and drink it and pass out.

We'd stay under that hot sun, next to the crumbling sand castles, until it went down and my skin felt rubbed raw. And then we'd drive home.

I'd keep my eyes on the solid traffic line we crossed before she'd jerk the car back into the right lane.

And she'd tell me how lucky I was to have a mom who loved me the way she loved me.

Something drips from my nose, and for a moment I wonder if I'm crying. I touch my eyes, but they're dry.

I wipe my nose with my arm.

It's blood.

The trickle comes faster until I can taste it on my lips, metallic from the iron in it. I think about having iron in me but not feeling strong. I lean forward, watch my blood drip onto the dirt.

Blood and dirt. It somehow seems important; it somehow seems amazing. I watch as more blood flows faster from my nose and drips onto the dusty earth. I can't believe I'm made of blood and metal and vessels and veins. And then I think my heart must have burst from being squeezed so hard. And now I'm bleeding out.

I see the gas station ahead. Time moves strangely. First it drips, then it flows. I open the door.

"Jesus Christ," he says, and I think it's funny because I'm not Jesus Christ.

The world is black and suddenly he is there, holding napkins to my face, pressing them against my nose.

I know him, but I can't remember his name. I watch little red hot dogs burning as they turn and turn on metal rollers.

He pulls the napkins away from my face. The red on white is beautiful. I want to make paper flowers with them. I reach for them, red paper flowers, for me. But he pulls them out of my reach, presses them to my nose again.

"Why do you keep doing this? You don't know this sun. It's the devil."

"El diablo," I say. He looks at me. I think I laugh.

He's wrong, though. The sun isn't the devil. It's glorious. It can make you forget, or at least remember in a way that doesn't hurt. The sun is a drug.

He leads me to the chair behind the counter. I sit and stare at the television as he goes to the cooler and pulls out water bottles. There are so many movies, so many DVDs stacked behind the counter. I try to read the titles even as the letters float and get blurry.

I watch as he comes toward me with a bottle of water. I wish he'd grabbed an orange soda to share with me. We could drink the liquid sun together. Maybe that way we could conquer it. Or maybe it would poison us.

We could be Romeo and Juliet. I know the thought is ridiculous as I think it, and I laugh again.

Romeo looks at me like I've lost my mind.

He hands me the bottle and I take a tasteless sip. No sun. Rivers. Clear, cool rivers.

He tells me to drink more, but slowly. I do. Like the other day, he trickles some water on my neck. I close my eyes.

I get lost in the colors that swirl behind my lids. I get lost in the mushy feel of my brain.

I feel a cold, wet touch on my arm.

"What's this?" Paulo asks. Paulo. His name and face appear in my head and I open my eyes, reeling back from shining waters and highways.

I look at the armband. "A black sock," I tell him.

"Well yeah, but why are you wearing it?" he asks.

I shrug.

"You don't know?" he asks. He leans closer to me, pulls at the sock softly, and unties it as the gas station door opens. An old man wearing a cowboy hat comes in.

"¿Qué pasa, Paulo?" the man calls out.

Paulo gets up, goes over to the register, and talks to the man. He reaches up for cigarettes and hands them to the man. I see their dark silhouettes against the light coming in through the smudged glass. A few more customers follow, trickling in one after the other. Paulo rings them up, speaks Spanish and English to them. He sounds the same but different in each language.

I think about language. I close my eyes and curl my tongue in my mouth, feeling for different languages that might have resided there if I lived somewhere else. Then I think about living somewhere else. How did I end up here? I could have lived in Sweden or Spain. I could have lived in South Africa or China. I think of Mexico, less than two miles down the road.

"¡Niña!" A woman's harsh voice pulls me from my thoughts. I open my eyes and see Paulo's grandmother standing in front of me, two jugs of water in either hand. "Are you okay?" she asks.

I nod. "Sí, sí. I'm fine," I say, feeling a little embarrassed. I look over at Paulo, who is bringing a box out of a back room. His grandmother stares at me for a moment longer.

"I'm all right," I say to her again. She doesn't look convinced, but she nods and says something I don't understand to Paulo before they both walk outside. I watch Paulo load the box and the jugs of water into the truck. I see a few of his grandmother's wooden crosses through the passenger-side window.

Paulo comes back into the store.

"Your grandmother must think I'm crazy," I mumble as we watch her drive away.

"My grandmother doesn't judge people on their journey," he says. "She knows what it is to have to overcome."

I'm about to ask him what he means, but then I see the truck turn off the main road suddenly, heading into the nothingness of the desert.

"Where's she going?" I ask, hypnotized by the blooming trail of dust the truck leaves behind.

"The desert. She leaves water and cans of food for those crossing the border. To help them survive," Paulo says. "And for those who don't, she marks the places where they crossed into the other world."

I watch the dust as his grandmother heads farther out. I want to go with her. I want to go deep in the desert. I want to cross into other lands.

I don't realize I've told Paulo I want to go to Mexico until I hear him say *You're crazy, no way I'm taking you across the border like this. . . .*

His words continue but he sounds far away and I feel so dizzy. I close my eyes and lean my head back for a moment. Each word he says is a pulsing white star behind my eyelids.

People come into the store, I think. I'm only half aware of the sound of their voices as the pulsing white stars behind my lids return with the words floating through my head. I try to make sense of my thoughts.

Someone once told me we're made of stars. I wonder how the stars that made me came together and ended up in my mother's womb. I think about the stars that make up the bear in the sky. I see him dancing. I imagine me being born.

A shooting star in a blacker-than-black sky.

The radio on the other side of the counter suddenly makes a staticky sound and comes to life, and the delicate tinkling notes of a piano fill the gas station. I open my eyes, I think, but the room is empty.

I look back, between the radio and the television, but it's not the movie. It's definitely the radio.

And it's definitely Patsy Cline.

I stare at the radio, because it must be wrong. Nobody plays Patsy Cline anymore. It wasn't on a moment ago; nothing was on a moment ago. But it's playing now.

I look up and through the large front window. I see the bear emerging, far away, from the hot desert. His black fur glistens under the sun. He runs, his paws pounding the earth. Sending orange mushroom clouds up to the sky with each step.

I'm mesmerized.

I shake. There are earthquakes. A dust storm rumbling through. The world is brown and orange.

He will crumble the earth. The mountains will fall and bury me.

I wait.

I lose sight of him in the darkening day, but moments later the door opens and he stalks through it.

I look at the red blooming flowers now in my hand. He smelled my blood. I offer him the paper flowers, but he shakes his head and sways to Patsy's smooth, steady voice.

"Look what's on, a movie about Patsy Cline. Watch it with me, baby," Mom said. She patted her bed.

Her words were only a little slurred. And she looked at me with sad eyes, so I did.

I climbed into bed next to her, like I was ten years old again even though I was already fourteen. And I watched what was left of the movie.

She scooted closer to me, wrapped an arm around my shoulder, and tucked me closer to her. I hated that because it was fake. It was strange for her to hold me like that. But I wouldn't have resented it so much if she'd hugged me when I wanted her to, if instead of pushing me away like she usually did, she'd done this. *Why do you have to be such a terrible daughter?* I asked myself while looking at her blotchy, unhappy face, at her hand clutching my arm like she couldn't bear to let me go. *Because everything, everything, was always on your terms.*

And then Patsy was getting beaten up.

And Mom's breathing got faster; her chest rose and fell and her heart thumped loud against my ear. I looked at her and saw tears in her eyes, but she shook her head and smiled at me. A *don't you worry* kind of look. But she held me so tight, I could feel the bruises forming on my arm.

She asked me to get her some tissues. By the time I came back, she was curled up into herself, sobbing so hard she could hardly breathe.

I just watched her. I stood there and watched. And I hated her because she drank too much and got so emotional and even love was on her terms. We couldn't even watch a movie together.

"You should drink less," I whispered. And I tossed the tissues on the bed and went to my room.

I open my eyes. The bear is gone. The sun is going down and I don't know if I've been sleeping, but I feel like I have. Paulo is turning off the television, grabbing some books, and telling me he'll take me home.

. . .

"Your name isn't Ruby," he tells me as the truck jostles us over rocks and holes in the earth.

I shrug.

"My grandmother. She knows everything about everyone." He looks at me sideways. "So what is it?"

I see myself taking a swig of the orange soda, stuffing pink gum into my pockets. Why hadn't he stopped me?

"Why'd you ignore me the other day?" I ask.

He smiles. Shakes his head and laughs. "You hardly talk at all. When you do, you give me a fake name. You come to the store delirious or bleeding or stealing, and the first thing you ask me is why I *ignored* you the other day?"

I don't answer. He looks over again, but I stare at the road ahead.

"I don't know," he says, like all of that was no big

deal. "I figured there was a reason for the fake name. Then when you showed up, I thought I'd let you talk if you wanted to. But you didn't, so . . ." He shrugs. "You were gone before I could decide what it meant."

I keep my eyes straight ahead, but I remember his face that day he and his grandmother gave me tea. So I know when he smiles, it is kind. And his eyes are soft. And he reminds me of the kindness people used to show me before I decided it only made everything else, everything my mother was, sharper. Before I made myself into someone people didn't want to be kind to anymore.

I'm tired, and I try not to look over at him, but I do.

"My name is Dani," I tell him.

He smiles. "Are you sure?" I nod but look back out the window because I don't want to say too much.

He fills up the silence with general questions. Where am I from? What's Florida like? Did I live near the beach? He's never been to the beach.

And I answer him. Each answer feels strange and familiar. Like I'm talking about someone else. Like I'm somewhere else, in a past where I used to make friends.

When we get to Shelly's house, Paulo looks at me.

"So you going to show up again tomorrow? Steal pink gum? Or are you going to stop walking miles and miles in this heat?"

"I don't know," I tell him.

He gives me a funny look and I open the door and get out of the truck.

"Hey, listen," he says. I look at him and he taps the wheel. "I'm going into town tomorrow. Maybe you want to go. I mean, there's not much to do around here and, I dunno. Maybe you want a break? From the desert?"

I look at the desert around me. I want to ignore him, but I think about tomorrow. About the slashes on the calendar. Tomorrow will be yet another slash.

"Ten?" he says. "I'll come by in the morning. Around ten."

I wonder what it's even like, hanging out with someone who doesn't hate you. And I think, *Can I trust you?* It makes me laugh, the stupid thought. But Paulo thinks it means yes and I don't have anything left in me to tell him no.

"Cool." He smiles again. I turn to go inside and he suddenly asks, "Hey, why pink gum?"

I shrug. "They're pretty," I tell him. It's not a lie. They are pretty.

But they're also like the sun.
They explode in my head.

• • •

He shows up at ten, like he said he would, and we drive to town. The world outside the open passenger window passes quickly, sky so blue, immovable mountains, blurry brown and orange dirt. The earth's hot breath blows over us. I didn't know wind could blow so hot. It makes me think something is coming.

"I feel like I'm in a dream here," I say.

"In this place? You don't dream big, do you?"

"It just feels that way. I think if I leave, I'll never find it again." I feel strange, telling him that, and I wonder why I did.

He looks over at me. "Is that good or bad?"

"Both, I guess." I don't say any more. I lean my head against the window frame and we drive the rest of the way in silence.

It's beautiful, riding like this. The hot wind blowing over me. The way I become hypnotized by the passing earth.

I don't realize how much I've gotten used to the solitude of the desert until we enter Deming and everything seems too busy. People are going in and out of stores. Eating lunch. We stop at Walmart and Paulo leads the way, straight to the movies section.

"You like movies?" I ask him.

"You could say that."

He starts picking up this one and that one, telling me about the director and the plot of each. Telling me how popular movies tend to be violent because people like it, all the killing and things blowing up. "People get off on it. Violence. The fantasy of it."

I want to ask him what he means, but before I can make myself get the words out, he grabs a DVD from the shelf and says, "This is the one I was looking for. Come on, you want to get lunch?"

I shrug and we end up at a place that smells like grilled meat and has walls painted Southwestern yellow and orange.

"So . . . ," he says when we sit down. With us facing each other, I'm forced to look at his face, his light brown eyebrows and too-kind eyes. I try to think of something to say. But I feel unreal, like I'm still in the truck, the hot wind blowing over me, parts of me floating everywhere.

"So," I say back.

"So . . . ," he says, smiling. Like we're playing some sort of game.

The waitress comes and takes our drink order and leaves too quickly.

"So, what were you saying?" he asks. He laughs at his own joke and because I don't, because I'm still wondering how I got here, he tells me he's kidding.

"I know," I tell him.

"You don't laugh much, do you?"

The waitress returns with our drinks and tosses two straws on the table.

I shrug. I don't know if I laugh a lot or not. I never thought about it. But then the image of the jackrabbit Shelly hit on the way home from the airport goes through my brain. It catches me off guard, that image from forever ago, and makes me laugh as I take a sip from my soda. It almost comes up through my nose.

"What?" Paulo says as I cough.

I shake my head.

"Tell me." His eyes are already laughing. He's making it easy for me because he wants to laugh. But I don't know if these are the kinds of thoughts you're supposed to share with somebody.

"You'll think I'm a terrible person." *You're a terrible daughter.* That's what she thought, isn't it? And I was.

And I thought she was a terrible mother. And she was.

We were both terrible.

I take another sip.

"I won't think you're terrible," he tells me. "I promise."

The waitress comes back, but we forgot to look at the menu, so she leaves again.

Finally, I tell Paulo about the jackrabbit. I watch his face the whole time, the crease in his brow that warns me to stop because I'm telling the story badly and it sounds stupid as I continue. But I go on, trying to explain the break dancing until he holds up a hand and says, "Wow . . ."

I don't know what to say. But then he smiles. "I'm just kidding. I mean, it's not as funny to me because it's one of those 'you had to be there' moments, but I can see how it *could* be funny."

"Thanks," I say. An uncomfortable heat crawls up my back and cheeks.

"No, I mean it. Like, there was this time . . ." He

stops and shakes his head. "This is a thousand times worse than your jackrabbit."

"Go on." I want him to tell me.

Finally, he wipes his hands on his jeans and leans forward. "Okay. So, it was years ago. There was this old lady, Doña Soledad, who used to live a couple of rows of trailers over. I never talked to her much, but she'd come visit my grandmother every now and then. She had a husband once, and a son who fell off a mountain when he was just a little boy."

The words tumble out of his mouth like nothing.

"What?"

"It's a sad story, but that's not the one I'm telling. God, I don't know. This is going to sound horrible."

He takes a deep breath. "So, the husband died a couple of decades ago, and the boy . . ." He gestures with his hand like it was so far in the past, it's not even relevant. "He died like fifty years ago and she's lived alone in her trailer ever since. But the lady was strong. She would walk and walk. It was weird. And she always wore black, like the little viejitas from the old days: head-to-toe black, black mantilla on her head, rosary around her neck, the whole thing. Anyway, she was a good lady."

The way he tells it, I can picture the woman.

"One day I start walking." He leans back. "You know, maybe something here makes people do stuff like that, walk aimlessly." He shakes his head. "Anyway, I was really bored and I'm beyond where all the trailers are and I'm kicking rocks around and there's kind of this little ditch on the side of the road that slopes down."

I nod, because I know exactly the spot he's talking about.

"And something, *something*, just makes me look over." He pauses. "And that's when I see her."

"Who?"

"Doña Soledad."

"In the ditch?"

He nods. "Yep, flat on her back, feet pointed to the sky, her body stiff and straight, and her hands folded on her stomach like she's already in a coffin."

"No . . ."

He nods, assuring me he's telling me the truth. "Yes. She was just there and . . ." He hesitates.

"What?" I ask him.

"It was her face. . . ."

I imagine the old woman's face, sad and cracked and brown like the bark of a tree. But maybe it was torn apart.

"What about it?" I whisper, bracing myself for the picture he's about to paint.

But instead, a smile tugs at the corners of Paulo's mouth. "Her face . . ." He looks down and I can see that he's smiling, and he coughs like he's trying to suppress laughter from making its way out. He shakes his head, clears his throat.

"What about it?" I ask. "Tell me."

Just then the waitress returns.

"You guys going to order something?" she says, putting some chips and salsa on the table. "Today?"

Paulo orders a burger and I do the same, just because it's easier, just to get back to the story.

The waitress walks away and I look at him and wait.

"Her face looked like the Joker's," he whispers. "You know, that weird smile? It was crazy-looking and frozen on her face. She looked *just* like him. I mean, *just* like him."

He clears his throat, but I can tell he still wants to laugh. "She's this tiny little old lady I've seen forever and she's sweet. Doña Soledad was good people, but she's got this crazy Joker smile on her face and I started laughing. I knew I should be freaked out, but she's looking at me like she's laughing too. Like she's thinking, *Madre! What the hell just happened? I'm freaking dead!* So all I can do is laugh."

"That's horrible," I tell him, but I can see the scene he's describing. I can see it perfectly. And it almost does *seem* funny.

"I know." He tries to look serious, but laughs again and fiddles with his straw nervously. "She was nice."

Seeing Paulo try to control his laughter makes me smile. "I thought you hated people getting off on violence."

His laughter stops and he shrugs. "I do. But what

happened to Doña Soledad, that's not violence, that's dying. That's just life."

"Maybe," I say, but something is starting to swirl in my head and an image of my backyard that day flashes through my mind.

"Anyway, I know a ton of stories like that," he says. "And stories so sad, you think you'll break. You think they can't be real. . . ."

I feel something in my chest swelling, so big and fast I'm afraid my chest might crack open suddenly.

"But they are," Paulo continues. "They're real and they happened and, shit . . . they're tragic, you know." He searches my eyes, but I look away. "Even if people want to pretend that kind of shit doesn't happen. It does. Even if the rest of the world forgets the people it happens to. You know?"

I can feel my breathing coming faster and I want to put my finger over my lips and whisper *Shhhhhhhh*.

No, I want to put my hand over his mouth and tell him *Don't say another word. Not one more word.* And when he looks at me with a crazy, confused expression, wondering what the hell I'm doing, I want him to see, to recognize how close to the truth he has come. Even if part of me doesn't.

I don't say anything, though. The waitress brings the burgers and I pick up mine, take a bite, and chew, because then maybe I won't scream. I look out the window and try to figure out how to keep my chest from cracking open and spilling everything out. Pieces of me.

Paulo picks up his burger and eats and neither of us talks for a while.

"Anyway," he says finally. "That's why I'm always watching movies. I'm going to tell those stories."

I take a drink from my soda. Paulo keeps his eyes on me as he eats.

"I mean, I know what people think," he says between bites. "When they see me working at the gas station, they think I'm just this Mexican kid headed nowhere. But I'm observing everyone, taking in everything, teaching myself everything I can about film because I'm going to tell the stories that people ignore. Make movies that make people think." He taps a finger on the side of his head. "Make people really fucking think."

He stops suddenly. "Jesus, I've been talking about myself for the last ten minutes." He laughs under his breath. "I mean, what about you?"

I take a deep breath. "Me?"

"Yeah," he says. "You. What are you thinking?"

I don't know about me anymore. I swirl a fry in ketchup, think about everything he's said. "Sometimes," I say, looking into his eyes, "sometimes it feels like I've been electrocuted."

He takes a sip of his drink. Doesn't laugh. He nods. "Go on," he says.

"I feel the current running through me, to the very tips of my fingers, zapping everything inside, burning my scalp. And then, nothing. I think sometimes . . . life is violent," I tell him.

I see some sort of sadness and understanding in his face. His soft eyes get serious and he looks like he wants to ask me something, but he doesn't.

"Life *is* violent," he says.

I look out the window. I wonder what Meursault would think of all this.

I try to eat, but my throat feels closed up. I think I'm going to cry and I don't understand why. And I don't want to. Not ever. So I stare at the cars driving by outside, but then Paulo gets my attention.

"Hey," he says, "hey . . ." I look at him. He puts his arms out and acts like a pulse of electricity is traveling from one arm to another and back again. He shakes his head like he's in shock. I watch him and sort of laugh.

He does the robot. And it's pretty funny.

I laugh harder.

Then he's putting his hands up to his face, saying, "Madre, Paulo! What happened! I'm freaking dead!" And then we're both laughing, the faces of the Joker and a break-dancing rabbit running through our minds.

Somehow laughing feels like crying, so I keep laughing.

And when the bear appears, trying to distract me by pulling a Joker mask out from behind his back and over his face, then by twirling on his back and break-dancing, I ignore him. I keep my eyes on Paulo.

But the bear leans against the wall and waits for us. Follows us around town. To the grocery store. To the tire place to check about a replacement. To deliver some tea leaves to some lady Paulo's grandmother knows. He roars and trails behind us the whole time.

I try to focus on what Paulo is saying. I nod and resist turning to look at the bear, resist running away.

On the drive back to the desert, I hear him breathing, louder, until I look straight in the mirror at him in the backseat. Our eyes lock and he roars softly.

Don't forget me, he's saying. *You can't forget me.*

• • •

It's been fifty-five days since she died. This time I don't tell Shelly.

But I keep track because I'm weary of time. The way it goes too fast. Or not fast enough. I mark each day with a slash, just to make sense of it.

Sometimes Paulo drives here after work and we watch movies. He tells me about them, hits pause every five minutes and explains too much, but I don't mind. I like the sound of his voice. Sometimes I'm falling asleep and I can feel his grandmother squeeze my heart from far away. Sometimes I catch glimpses of Shelly's face and I see Mom.

Sometimes I think she's come back for me.

Sometimes Paulo is asking me about me, what I like, and I can't answer him. I don't remember. I can only remember what I hated.

Today, Shelly put a pack of socks on my bed. And a T-shirt with the tags still on. It's just socks, I tell myself, and a stupid T-shirt with a rock star who is probably aging and cursing at having his image go for $7.99 at Walmart.

But something about the little stack on the neatly made bed I did not make myself moves me. I swallow the lump in my throat and know I should go knock on her door and thank her.

But I pick up *The Stranger* and read.

"Come watch a movie," I hear after a while. It's Shelly standing in my doorway, looking in but not entering.

I look at her. She even stands like Mom.

I put down the book. Meursault is on the beach; the sun beats down on him. Shelly waits until I say, "Okay," and I dog-ear the page and get up.

I head to the living room with the image of the beach and the sun and the sand and the water in my head. I can't stop thinking of Meursault, standing there, his head exploding and hurting from the blinding sun. I know if he closes his eyes, he'll see white-hot flames pulse through his mind instead. No relief if he opens his eyes. No relief when he closes them. The sun, just beating him up without punches, without knives, without guns, just its inescapable brightness and unbearable heat.

I feel bad for leaving him there like that, to suffer until I get back, but that's how I leave him. Then I picture Meursault and me, him at the beach, me in the desert, both of us walking under the assaulting sun. And I think it's not fair how he can easily stay numb. I wonder if he'll struggle to stay numb. I wonder if Paulo's grandmother squeezes his heart.

I walk down the dark hallway to the living room where Shelly waits, a bowl of popcorn in her hands.

"You all right?" she asks as I squint at the brightness coming in through the windows.

I shrug. "Just tired."

I sit down on the other side of the couch, leaving plenty of room between us.

"I've picked out a couple of movies. You can choose," she says, placing the bowl of popcorn on the center pillow and reaching down to grab a small stack of DVDs from the floor near her feet. I reach over and grab a handful of buttery popcorn.

"Not much of a choice. They're all old. *Stand by Me* and *The Shawshank Redemption* are the best ones. I picked up most of these from the dollar bin."

I look down at the pile and wonder where she dug them up from. I've been all over this house and never seen them.

"We used to have videotapes," Shelly says. She

looks like she's remembering something, but shrugs it away and holds up *Shawshank*.

"This one?"

"Sure."

"Where are the videotapes?" I ask. The popcorn crunches in my mouth. A thin shell of a kernel jams itself between my teeth.

"Gone. Those don't hold up very well over time," Shelly says, putting the DVD in.

I've seen *Shawshank* tons of times since it's one of those movies that's always on television. But I don't tell Shelly, because I don't mind watching it again.

Shelly sits next to me. "We used to watch movies together," she says, not taking her eyes off the screen.

I look over at her and I don't know whether or not I want her to tell me more. I don't know whether I want to know anything or everything. Or whether I'd even believe the things she might say. I haven't caught her in any lies, but maybe she'd tell me about Mom when she wasn't who I knew, the woman who stabbed me with sharp words, clobbered me with a heavy hand, hated me so much I could feel it.

"Sometimes it was just the two of us, but other times we watched movies with our mom, your grandmother." This time Shelly does look at me, and the expression on her face reminds me of the bear, the way he roars so I'll notice him.

A picture flashes in my head. I don't recognize my

mom. It's somebody else, someone who watched movies with her sister and her mother. I wonder what her favorite movie was. I don't want to know, I try not to ask, but the words come out. Shelly flinches only slightly, like some invisible hand just pinched her, and answers before I can tell her *Stop! I made a mistake! I don't want to know!*

"*The Wizard of Oz*," she says. Her eyes want to stay hard, no-nonsense, but they betray her. Because in them I see a wave of love, of regret and memory. "I'll tell you anything you want to know. About your mom, our lives. I'll be honest."

I return my gaze to the screen.

She tries again. "One time . . ."

I shake my head. *No, no, all I want to know is the version of her that I already know.* Mom's face in anger, frustration, disappointment, apathy. Because that's who she was. That's who she was to me. I close my eyes, hope Shelly doesn't go on.

She doesn't.

We watch the movie and I let it fill my head and I wonder what it would be like to be locked up that way. I think of having four walls around me all the time, and I think that would make me crazy. But then I think, maybe there is some kind of messed-up comfort in those four walls, because out in the open, you're vulnerable. Out in the open, there are bears.

I'm thinking too much. A part of me wishes I were

watching this with Paulo and all his talk about camera shots and angles and the meaning of every hidden thing directors put in movies.

We watch Andy retch as he swims through a tunnel of feces to escape the prison during a thunderstorm.

It's the water that makes that scene what it is. Andy going through shit first, and then, the cleansing of water. Water pouring from the sky, pouring over him, washing him clean, like God himself is part of the escape plan.

I probably wouldn't make it. I think of slushing through the feces and I know I wouldn't. I'd probably stay in my cell. I'd probably die there or wait to be killed.

The movie ends and Shelly says she's going to her room. She turns off the lights, locks the doors. She says goodnight, but she stays in the doorway and looks at me.

"Dani . . . ," she says, and her voice has something in it that makes my heart ache.

"I'm okay," I tell her before she can say anything more.

But she stays, like she's watching over me. Like she can't let me out of her sight.

"Really," I tell her.

"Okay," she says. "Sleep tight." I watch as she turns slowly and walks down the hall. I wait for the click of her door closing, but it doesn't come.

I restart the movie and blue-white light fills the room.

I watch until Morgan Freeman's voice sounds far away, but then I feel electricity in the air. I open my eyes and see the bear standing next to me, the blue-white light from the television flickering on his glistening black fur. He leans down and roars gently in my ear. Then he walks over to the door.

What do you want? I ask him.

He looks back at me, as if he's been waiting for that question. He nods, and then motions with his paw for me to follow.

I sit up. Maybe if I follow his directions he'll leave. Or maybe he'll kill me.

I don't know.

I think of Andy in that tunnel. I think of Meursault on the beach. I think of water and sun.

I think of Ruby Falls.

The bear has opened the door. I hear the gravel under his paws. I hear the door to the barn open. I'm afraid Shelly will wake up, see him, and know that I've brought him here.

I look toward Shelly's room. If I screamed, would she come running?

There *is* something out there. But I don't want to know what it is. And I don't think I can go.

Besides, Meursault is still on the beach. And, God, if I were struck with heat and exhaustion and blinding sun, I'd want someone to come for me.

So I get up.

I turn off the television.

And head to my room. I look down the hall at Shelly's open bedroom door and I want to whisper her name, just to see if she'd hear me. Just to see if she'd come.

Would you face the bear with me? I want to ask.

But I don't. I go in my room and close the door.

. . .

"Hey, I'm taking you somewhere," Paulo says one morning, smiling at me when I open the door.

"Where?"

"Across the border. To Mexico."

"Mexico? Why?" I ask.

He gives me a funny smile. "You said you wanted to go. The other day? Remember?"

I don't. "Mexico?"

He laughs. "Yeah, come on," he says. "Or what, you wanna stay in here the rest of your life or something?"

The world is so big, Dani, and we're not going to stay hidden in corners of it like roaches. We're not roaches. We're not vermin.

"You have a passport?"

"Yeah . . . ," I say slowly.

"Let's go, then," he says. "Just for a little while. We'll stay close to the border."

He smiles again and the eagerness in his face makes me say, "Okay."

I grab my wallet and passport. When I get back, Paulo's already in his truck, the tape deck playing some music I've never heard before.

"What's this?" I ask him.

He shrugs. "Just an old band my dad liked," he says. "His favorite."

I listen to the music and the words don't make sense to me, but there's a vulnerability to the singer's voice that makes me sorry the ride to the border is so short. When Paulo pulls into the parking lot of a gift shop on the U.S. side, he explains it will be easier to walk across than to drive.

"We don't have to deal with them checking the truck when we come back."

I nod like I know what's going on, and follow.

We walk by U.S. agents, then Mexican agents, and they just watch us.

"Don't we have to tell them anything?" I ask.

Paulo laughs. "Nobody gives a shit if you're leaving the U.S. to go to Mexico," he says. "Only if you're trying to come in."

Paulo reaches for my hand, which feels strange but comforting. I look down and notice how much longer his fingers are than mine, his nails square and broad. Looking at his fingers makes me want to bring his hand up to my cheek. But I loosen my grip and he lets go.

"So this is Mexico," I say, stating the obvious the

way you do when you don't know what to say. It feels different somehow, being here, on this side of the border, but also the same. I remember now, telling Paulo I wanted to come here. But I don't remember why.

"This is it," he says, "the evil of the world, the pain in the side of the USA."

I feel guilty and idiotic for some reason and I think Paulo notices, because he just shakes his head and says, "Forget it, come on."

We walk toward a pink building with a sign that reads THE PINK STORE.

The first thing I see when we enter are skeleton dolls, laughing skeleton dolls playing guitars, dancing, red roses in their hair. Paulo stares at one.

"They're cool," I tell him.

He picks the figure up. "My mother . . . she used to wear a rose in her hair. Her name was Rosa." He touches the red rose in the skeleton's hair, puts the figure back on the shelf carefully, and looks at something else down the way.

I don't know if he wants me to ask about Rosa or not. But I don't want to be reminded of mothers, so I pretend he didn't say anything and focus instead on the store, the wooden tops and postcards in a basket. The postcards have images of old-fashioned-looking guns, of women dressed in colorful skirts. There's jewelry, turquoise and pink necklaces that look like candy, and rings that look like they've been carved from ancient rocks and picked out of the sides of mountains, like the ones Doña Marcela wears. There are tiny bottles of liquor and paper fans. And, strung from the ceiling, banners made of paper cutouts in the same colors as those little squares of gum.

"Come on," Paulo says, leading me out of the front room. We enter another room, full of crosses on the wall. Then we go to the back room, full of beautiful plates and bowls, mugs, and vases.

Paulo goes down one aisle and I go down the other, looking at all the bowls.

I look up, see Paulo staring at me through the open shelf between the two aisles.

He is disheveled, strands of hair flying in every direction. His shirt never lies right on him; it always looks like he's buttoned it one button off, but he hasn't. His eyes, which change depending on the light, are the darkest shade of gray right now.

"What?" I ask him when he doesn't look away.

"Nothing," he says, expecting the question, but keeping his gaze on me.

"Stop staring at me," I tell him.

"Why?"

"It's uncomfortable." I stare back at him, keep my eyes on him just the same way he keeps them on me. "Do you like it? Being uncomfortable?" I ask when I see him shift slightly.

He shrugs. "I don't mind."

"Sure you don't."

He laughs and looks away. I concentrate on a sugar

bowl decorated with drops of pink paint, but I can feel him watching me.

"Know what happens if you don't talk about it?" Paulo says suddenly, quietly, so quietly I'm not sure he's said anything. I look at him again.

"It eats you alive," he says. "It starts here." He puts his hand on his chest, on his heart. "And it starts feeding on this, little by little, eating away at your heart until it kills it."

I stare at him. His eyes catch the overhead light and shimmer, but his face is serious.

"Then it stops pumping blood to your body; your limbs get cold and go numb. You die because you have no heart."

I feel a little light-headed, like I got up too quickly. I focus on the sugar bowl again and run a finger over the pink dots. Paulo goes on.

"My grandmother says you can grow a new heart. Do you believe that?" he asks me, continuing down the aisle. I follow on the other side.

I shake my head. "No."

He shrugs. "It's hard. But you can grow another one. Or I'd be dead."

He walks to the end of the aisle and I follow on my side until we meet at the end. He takes my hand, and something about his touch after what he's said makes me feel a squeeze in my chest.

We walk around until we are bored and have looked at everything and are back at the front of the store. He grabs a cardboard box from a display near the register and a soda from the cooler next to it. The box looks like tarot cards until I read the name. *Lotería.* Paulo pays, but just as we are about to leave, I see a postcard with a landscape of little houses upon little houses on the side of a mountain and big, yellow bubble letters that say MEXICO! Next to the postcard are miniature crosses like the ones on the wall. I pick one up and also the postcard and pay for both.

When we leave, I turn to look at the skeleton with the rose in her hair. She smiles her skeletal smile at me and I wonder what happened to Paulo's mother and father.

We walk up and down a couple of streets. Share the glass bottle of orange soda. The colors of stores and houses and shacks and churches along the streets are strange. Some so bright and others so weathered, like they've been washed out and rotted by too much rain.

We walk like we know where we're going, but we don't. Neither of us. I want to lean on Paulo and feel his cheek against mine. I want to whisper the truth to him.

We're orphans, I want to tell him. Our mothers and fathers are gone. The ones who were supposed to love us the most.

But he's looking at a church and the people filing out and he pulls me toward it.

We go inside and the stained glass is so beautiful it

makes me want to cry, and Jesus is up on the cross in pain, and we sit in the back and try to feel God. But I think of Paulo and I think of me and I wonder if God is real. I look at the cross, then at Paulo.

"I remember riding around with my dad in his truck. Listening to those songs he liked to sing."

The quiet of the church, and the light shining behind the stained glass, makes me forget to be careful.

"What happened?" I ask.

Paulo doesn't answer, so I immediately feel like I shouldn't have said anything. What business is it of mine? He's never asked about my mom. Neither of us has talked about our parents at all.

"Life," he says. "Life happened."

He doesn't say anything more and I don't ask. But a moment later, he continues. "He was a good man. But one day somebody got him confused with someone who wasn't good. That was it. That was his crime . . . happens all the time."

Paulo looks at the crucifix in front of us and goes on.

"My mom was always telling him we should stay in the U.S. with my grandmother. But my dad was a proud man. Proud of his country. Proud of his family's land and their horses and cows." He laughs softly. "He wanted to stay in Mexico, live an honest life. He'd say, 'What for? They don't even think we're human over there.' I'd hear them talking about it, my mom telling him things were getting bad and that we should go. She was worried that something might happen to me."

I stay quiet and Paulo keeps talking.

"So he says to her one day, 'Okay . . . we'll go.'" Paulo shakes his head. "I know that was hard for him." He shrugs. "I think he just sensed something."

He looks over at me, trying to see if I understand. I do. I want to tell him I sensed the bear. That I'd always sensed it. That he'd been coming for us forever. I open my mouth. I try to tell him. I try to tell him something, anything, about my mom. But I can't.

"You okay?" he asks.

I swallow, tell myself to answer. "Fine," I manage. But really, I can't get the images out of my head. Of bears and water and a man who was good and the women who were once our mothers but are now gone.

"I'm fine," I say again. He doesn't believe me.

"We should go," he says.

Outside, Paulo looks at the dirt road ahead and then turns around, as if he's searching for something. I want to tell him *You're searching for your father. For your mother. You'll always be searching for them. Because we are little pieces of them . . . because once their wombs were our home.* But I say nothing and Paulo leads the way to the border.

He holds my hand and we go to the official-looking building and we show our passports and we cross the border, and we get back in his truck, and we drive.

But it feels like no matter what direction we go, or how long we drive, or what borders we cross, we're never really going home.

• • •

It's been seventy-two days since Mom died.

At night, I make another slash on the calendar and then take out the postcard I've kept in my book. MEXICO!

I get up in the dark house and head to the kitchen, where Shelly leaves the computer. I wonder what I would tell her if she woke up and saw the glow of the screen on my face. Would I say I'm looking up the address of the cemetery? Would I say I'm sending my mother a postcard?

I find the address, write it down. Back in my room I stare at the blank space for a message.

I put the postcard away in the pages of *The Stranger.* Then get up and take it out again.

I can't think of anything I'd say to her, and then words crowd my mind.

Dani was here.

Were you ever here?

Why'd you keep all this a secret?

Who were you?

Did I know you?

Did you love me?

I look down at my writing, writing that doesn't

even seem like my own. And then I hear him, outside my window. Roaring softly.

"What more do you want?" I whisper to him. He roars again and I reach over to turn off the light, but before I do, I write one more thing.

Are you sending the bear?

. . .

"Let's go register you at the high school," Shelly says to me in the morning.

I look over at her.

"I've got copies of your records, birth certificate, all that stuff." She holds up a large envelope. "The child services lady sent everything to me. School starts in two weeks."

Two weeks?

School? The whole idea of it seems strange. Of people in classrooms being taught theories and equations that could never save them from bears, or airplanes falling from the sky, or the bad luck of looking like a not-good man.

I'm about to nod, but I look at the envelope. Me, in that envelope, just a bunch of dates and grades and places I've been. Just facts. I think about Meursault.

If Shelly told him he had to register for school, he would simply get on that yellow bus and let it take him wherever it wanted. Because what did it matter? What did anything matter? It would deliver him to a strange school where others would instantly sense he was different but he wouldn't care. And he would go down the halls saying nothing. He would sit in the back of each class, observe everyone and everything, and then get up and go to the next class.

But I don't want to deal with teachers and assignments, with eating lunch at a certain hour, with fighting my way through crowded halls. *Don't think about it*, I tell myself. *Be like Meursault.*

"Did you hear me?" Shelly asks.

I think of myself at the steps of a new school with crowds of people swallowing me up. I think of the strange looks you get when you're new.

But I also see myself at the steps of a crumbling school. I think of myself in empty classrooms, long after I should have graduated. I think of the bear there with me. Still with me.

"I can't . . . ," I tell her. "I really can't. Please . . ."

She puts the envelope down. "Dani . . ."

"Please . . . ," I beg her. And I don't know why it feels like so much depends on this. "It's not that I hate school, I promise. I was a good student."

"I'm supposed to make you go. This is the role I have, right? I mean, that's what I'm supposed to do." She looks at me like I have the answers.

I shake my head. "No . . ."

She takes a deep, controlled breath.

"'I'll check into online stuff," I tell her. "People do that all the time now. Or I'll get my GED."

We stay that way forever, like a painting hanging in a museum. Untitled. At first glance you would wonder why the hell anyone would paint something so boring. But maybe someone would see the look in Shelly's eyes.

Would see the bear lurking in the hallway.

Would see a hand squeezing my heart.

Shelly shakes her head. "You have to go," she says.

I look at her. I know her mind is made up. I give up the fight.

• • •

The bus picks me up in front of a playground that seems out of place here. Shelly drives me to the bus stop even though I insist I can walk.

When I get out of the truck and sit on the low brick wall surrounding the playground, I expect her to drive away. But she sits in the car and watches me.

The two kids I saw walking in the desert are there, too. The boy looks at me. He's small and thin.

"You're Paulo's girl, right?" he asks.

"What?"

"I've seen you with him," he tells me. "You're his girl."

"That don't make her his girl," the girl says. She has long, dark brown hair, and when the sun catches strands of sparkling red, it's the color of cherry cola. "Don't mind him," she tells me. "He's always looking for a girlfriend, trying to figure out who's available, who's taken. Plus you're new. That got him interested right away."

"Shut up," he tells her.

She laughs and turns back to me. "I'm Jessie. What grade you in?"

"Senior," I tell her.

"Shit, that's messed up, having to move here your senior year."

I nod.

"You live with your aunt, right?" She nods in Shelly's direction.

I look toward the truck. I can't see Shelly because of the glare on the window. I wonder if she's looking at me.

"Yeah, I've seen you around, you and Paulo," the girl says, like she knows something about me. "Are you guys like a thing?"

I feel my cheeks getting warmer. "Just friends . . ."

"Okay, okay," she says. "Sure you are." She looks at me and laughs. "He used to drive us to school last year when he was a senior, before his grandma's gas station got held up and he started working there more."

"It got held up?"

"Yeah, it was nothing. Wasn't anyone here anyway. No one around here would do that to Doña Marcela. Had to be someone passing through who didn't know her."

"Why?"

She shrugs. "Because she's always helping people, you know? But she's tough as hell, too. I mean, *I* wouldn't mess with Doña Marcela."

I think of Doña Marcela standing in front of me with those jugs of water in her hands. Her stern face somehow offering both softness and refuge. I picture her driving through the desert, hammering crosses into the desolate land, leaving food and water for strangers on their journey.

Journeys of survival.

Paulo said something else about journeys, but I can't remember what.

Jessie interrupts my thoughts. "Don't go thinking there are always holdups around here or anything, though." She shrugs and rolls her eyes. "It's not like we're in shoot-outs all hours of the day the way people imagine."

"I wasn't thinking that. . . ."

"Anyway, you like it here?" she goes on.

"I . . ."

"I'm just joking," she says. "This place sucks."

"It's not that bad . . . ," I tell her.

"Hmm, if you say so. But I've lived here all my life and I can't wait to leave."

The boy looks up. "Shut up, yo," he tells her.

"Why? It's true. I'll go to Dallas or something. Get away from this fucking place. Sorry you got dumped here. But you'll probably leave too, right? First chance you get?"

I shrug.

"I would," she says. "I mean, I totally am. Gonna get an education and become something."

"Shut up!" the boy says again.

"Calm down, Chicken," she tells him. "You can live with me once you're done."

"Don't call me chicken," he tells her.

"Nickname," she says to me. "It's cuter in Spanish."

He shakes his head.

The bus comes and we get on.

There are only a few other kids on the bus and it's a lot quieter and calmer than I would've guessed. The other kids look up at me and then go back to what they were doing.

Chicken walks down the aisle toward the back. When I try to take a seat up front, Jessie tugs at my arm and says, "Uh-uh, come on. You don't want to look like some uppity white girl."

I follow her and we sit in the back. "Just stay away from this one," she says, pointing to the kid sitting behind us next to Chicken.

He looks up and rolls his eyes at her.

"Watches porno on his phone," she says loudly.

"Suck it, Jessie! It was one time!"

"Yeah, yeah . . . one time, whatever. I'm going to tell your mama, you little pervert," she says, but she's laughing and smacks him on the head.

He sucks his teeth and shakes his head. "Don't," he tells her.

"If you're good I won't."

Jessie chitchats some with other kids as we ride, but mostly she talks to me. She tells me that Chicken is scared she'll leave him behind for good since he doesn't bother to hit the books. She tells me he has learning disabilities. She tells me he could still go to a community college near where she'll move. Or he could study a trade that would make him good money, like auto repair. And then they can both get their parents out of here. Jessie talks a lot, but it's not annoying.

"Anyway, I mean, I don't want to end up living here. Or Mexico. No offense to my parents or anything," she says.

"Hey, hey, there's nothing wrong with Mexico!" one girl calls over.

"Shut up, I'm not saying there is," Jessie tells her.

"Just don't go giving another gringa a bad impression," she says.

"I'm not! Chill out."

"I'll die in Mexico," the girl says. She gives me a hard look. I nod because I don't know what else to do.

Jessie rolls her eyes. "You were born here," she says to the girl.

The girl shakes her head. "Like that makes a difference."

The boy next to her says, "It does if you're one of the little baby skeletons they find in the desert, or one of the kids who gets eaten by coyotes while trying to cross just because the shit at home is even worse."

"You don't have to tell me babies die, okay? I know. I'm just saying this place doesn't want us. Even though we were born here. They want to deport our asses to Mexico no matter what dirt we were born on. Because we're brown. But hey, if you want to bust your ass getting all As just so some asshole thinks all you do is scrub toilets and then calls the migra on you, then go for it. Good luck with that, chavo. Good luck."

The boy looks down, and then out the window.

Jessie turns to me, raises her eyebrows. "Anyway," she says, taking a deep breath and looking at me. "What about you? Where did you move from? Why are you here? Come on, this ride is like an hour long and we talk."

She looks at me, waiting. I think for a minute about what I can tell her. "I lived in Florida," I say finally. She waits for more. "With my mom. I lived there with my mom. Then I moved here because . . . she died."

It sounds weird to say it. I can't quite believe I did until Jessie looks at me all sad.

"Oh," she says. "I'm sorry."

"She wasn't . . . that great," I say before I can stop myself. I'm afraid to look at Jessie, to see the way she might be looking at me now. I wish I could take it back.

I glance at her, but her face remains soft and sad, like she understands. "Still, she was your mom," she says.

I look away fast and focus on the mirror at the front

of the bus, the one reflecting the bus driver's frizzy hair and sweaty forehead.

Because, yes, she was my mom.

. . .

When we get to school, Jessie tells me where my first class is. The school is not very big, a lot smaller than most of the schools I've gone to, so I don't feel totally overwhelmed. I had a quick tour of it when I registered with Shelly, so I have an idea where I'll be going throughout the day.

I head to my first class, passing him in the hall. I hardly pay attention at first, but I know he's there, painted on the wall and looking at me. A great black bear staring at the hall of students, his mouth open in one never-ending roar.

Shelly had stood frozen when she saw it. Said she'd forgotten the school mascot, and I thought then about telling her how I see the damn bear all the time. How he followed me all the way here from Florida and I wasn't sure how long he was going to stick around or why. But I didn't say anything. And she shook her head and walked out and I followed her.

I have only a couple of credits left to graduate because somehow I need fewer credits here than at my last school. So study hall and office assistant take up two of my classes.

The office assistant job has me at a desk that looks

right out at that bear. For an hour we stare at each other.

What do you want? I ask him. *What do you want?*

The rest of my classes are easy enough: AP English, sociology, phys ed, Spanish II, and film. I couldn't believe there was actually a film class, and when the guidance counselor suggested it, I thought at least I'd have that to look forward to.

When I walk into Mr. Diaz's class, he jokes with us, saying if we only took this class because we thought we'd be watching films all year, we were only half right.

Mr. Diaz wears slacks and a jacket and tie and his dark hair is combed very neatly. He tells us a little bit about the program, how he had to fight to get a class like this into the school, had to make his case to the school board because they thought film study was irrelevant in a school like this, even though he knew *this is exactly the kind of school where we need a film class!* And now his students are entering film festivals and making more films, and he knew one day, no doubt, *one of you, or many of you, will be accepting an Oscar.*

He tells us that by the end of the year, we'll be making our own films, and to get us motivated, he shows a couple of short films from some of his past students.

He turns off the lights. The first one is about a woman running away from a camera. As soon as it's over, I want to see it again. We talk about it, but then

Mr. Diaz moves on to the next one, about an old man and his shoes. We talk about that before he shows us a third.

This one starts by zooming in on a water faucet on the side of a small cement house. The water is dripping.

It cuts to a shot inside a vehicle. A guy wearing sunglasses drives through the desert.

Then the inside of a home, a woman making coffee. And this shot is weird, because you feel like you are the woman as you watch her hand stir the sugar into the coffee.

Back to the water faucet. Water dripping.

Then the guy again.

Back in the kitchen, the woman spills the coffee, and it drips over the counter and to the floor. She looks annoyed, throws the spoon on the counter, and begins wiping the mess up with a kitchen towel.

A guy comes into the kitchen from the hall. He is shirtless and disheveled, but he smiles at the woman as he shakes his head and says something. But the audience can't hear his words. In fact, it's at this point that you notice the soft drip-drip sound that has been in the background the whole time. It gets louder.

The woman shakes her head and looks amused, and she smiles too.

She walks into the hall, looks toward a room.

The water drips louder.

Then the car stops in front of the house and now

the camera angle is from the viewpoint of the guy with sunglasses.

He knocks on the door.

The water drips louder. And the image of the water faucet comes back onto the screen. This time the camera stays on the dripping water for ten drops and each drop is violently loud, like a bullet.

Then there's a shot of the guy driving away.

The door is open and the man and woman are on the floor, covered in blood.

The camera focuses on the doorway the woman had looked at earlier, and pans out. The water drops are soft again, and then the gruesome tableau goes to black.

The room is silent. The bell rings, making us all jump. Mr. Diaz says softly that we'll discuss it tomorrow.

I feel a cramp in my heart.

I think of Paulo.

• • •

By the time the hot air is whipping at my face on the bus ride home, I'm almost glad Shelly forced me to go. School breaks up the days.

The ride home is louder. Everyone is yelling and Jessie is sharing her headphones with Yolanda, the girl who is going to die in Mexico, and I just watch. I watch all of them because somehow they make me feel less like I'm floating. These are the faces I'll see for a while.

"How was your first day?" Yolanda yells when she catches me looking at her.

I shrug. "All right." I don't tell her how I walked to the cafeteria and picked up my lunch and brought it back to the office to eat at the desk where I sat staring at the bear. Maybe if I stared at him long enough, I'd figure out what he wanted.

She holds one of Jessie's earbuds to her ear and nods her head to the beat of the music. "That's good!" she yells. "But hey, if anybody gives you trouble, just let me know." Her wavy hair whips over her face, gets caught in her red lipstick. She doesn't bother to smooth the hair away. Instead she keeps nodding to the music, lets her hair get wilder, cover her completely, so she gets lost in it and the music.

A part of me is glad to have crossed paths with Jessie and Chicken and Yolanda. They made the day easier. And I realize I'm not afraid of school. I wasn't even afraid if anyone gave me any trouble.

Because I felt like the bear, quiet and powerful. And like I could tear anyone limb to limb if I had to.

When the bus comes to a stop, Jessie, Chicken, and I get off. Sitting where Shelly's truck was this morning is Paulo's truck.

He waves and Jessie nudges me. "Just friends," she whispers as Chicken runs over to Paulo. Jessie and I follow him.

"I'll give you a ride home," he says to me. "You guys, too," he says, nodding at Chicken and Jessie.

They jump in the bed of the truck, then tap the window when they're settled in.

Paulo pulls away from the curb and looks over at me. "Hey," he says.

"Hey," I answer.

I feel funny suddenly, like Paulo knows somehow about Jessie's teasing. Like it's made things different between us. Or maybe because until she said something, I didn't think about it much.

Paulo drives toward his house, then past it, and down a couple of roads on the grid of mobile homes. He slows in front of one with a green awning. It's pretty, carefully decorated with pots of flowers and rocks in the front yard.

Jessie and Chicken get out and yell "Thanks" to Paulo and "See you tomorrow" to me. I wave.

"So, how was it?"

"Fine," I tell him, and start to break down the day since it gives me something to talk about which feels safer than riding in silence. If I stop talking, I'm certain he'll feel the awkwardness I feel. He listens, and when I tell him about the film class, he smiles.

"Mr. Diaz! That was my favorite class," he says. "He's a cool guy. He's actually the one who got me into making movies."

"We have to make a film by the end of the school year."

"Yeah, yeah . . . I remember," he says, smiling. "You'll love it."

He drives and I stare out the window for a while.

"He showed us a few student films today," I tell him, knowing what it will lead to.

He looks over at me. "Oh yeah?"

"One was a girl running . . ." He nods like he knows what I'm talking about. "Another had this old guy . . ." I watch the way the wind blows his hair. "And the last had"—*bullets and blood and*—"this dripping water faucet."

He nods, staring straight ahead. I wait for him to confirm or deny what I suspect, but he just keeps driving. I suddenly think how stupid it was for me to mention the film. Too personal. It wasn't fair of me to bring it up, flaunting that I'd seen it like some little kid who has been given somebody else's toy.

We're silent the rest of the ride home, but when we get to Shelly's, Paulo reaches over and grabs my hand. I don't want him to leave and I know he doesn't want to either. And it feels like one of us has to say something.

"Come inside for a while," I say finally, without looking at him.

He turns off the truck and I listen to the pebbles rolling under our feet as we walk up to the three wooden steps that lead to the front door. He's close behind me every step of the way, and when I put the key in the lock, turn the knob, I can feel him watching my hands. And then I can feel him leaning in close to me. I turn to look at him and he holds my gaze for a few seconds. His eyes remind me of water and fog and smoke.

Then I feel his lips on mine.

He tastes warm and the thrill of his kiss makes my chest feel full, like there's an ocean inside me with rolling waves. I pull him closer and both his hands are on my face and it feels amazing to be wanted. It feels like I'm loved, like I matter. I'll do anything to keep feeling this way. I don't want to let go. I want to be a part of him.

And something zaps in my brain. I see my mother and all those men by the pool, all the images of her kissing them, how she tried to keep their eyes on her when they'd already turned away. I see her red smile, her sleepy eyes. I see how those guys were fascinated by her but quickly became bored. And when they left, how she tried to make each one stay.

I pull away fast. My hands find his chest and push him back.

"What's wrong?" he says, but I just shake my head. I can't look at him; I don't want him to see her, Ruby, in me.

I won't be like her.

"Nothing," I tell him. "I just . . . Shelly . . . ," I say as an explanation, even though it's not one. I look up and past Paulo's shoulder, as if she might be coming down the road at any moment. He turns and then looks back at me but doesn't say anything. I go inside and he follows me.

"You want something to drink?" I can feel his eyes on me, I can feel the way he's trying to figure out what just happened as I take out a glass, fill it with water.

"No, I'm okay," he says. I take a sip as he walks around the kitchen, but there's nothing to look at.

"You know, I've never seen your room," he says suddenly.

I stare at him.

"I'm curious," he explains.

"About?"

"You." He walks through the entryway to the hall and I hear his footsteps as he goes searching for my room. I follow him and watch as he goes in, looks at the bare dresser, the suitcase still on the floor, and the pile of dirty laundry in the corner.

He holds up my copy of *The Stranger*. "Any good?" he asks.

"It's okay."

He nods. I stand by the door. The room is as bare as the landscape outside.

"You know what you need?" he says, leaning against the dresser and still looking around. "You need posters. I've got a couple of movie posters in my room." He looks at the suitcase and adds, "Unless you're anxious to get out of here?"

I shrug and follow his gaze. Even the clothes that I've washed have been packed away again.

I hadn't been able to unpack. But I also don't have plans to be anywhere but here. I think of getting through one hour, and then the next, until all the hours of the day are up. And somehow, the days pass.

"Come on," I tell him. I suddenly don't want him in my room. Thinking I'm as stupid as Ruby. That just because it seems like my heart wants to love him, like my lips want to kiss him, that I'll do what she did; play the same part, believe that he wants me,

he loves me,

he'll never leave me.

Until I believe it enough that I don't care what might happen.

I suddenly wish he were anywhere but here. I search for words to explain, because I think he deserves an explanation, but all I can say is "Get out."

"What?"

"Get out. I don't want you here. . . ."

He looks confused. "What the hell? I'm not . . ." He stares at me like he'll figure it out, and he thinks he has, because he nods like he knows, but he doesn't.

He walks past me, but the thing is I don't want him to leave. And I hate that I don't want him to go. I want to yell at him *Go!* I want him to stay. But I won't beg. I won't beg like my mother did. He's halfway down the hall.

"Paulo . . ."

He turns around and looks at me. "Hey, listen, I wasn't trying anything." He shakes his head. "I mean, you get in my truck; you tell me you've seen my movie, right? So you know, *you know*. . . ." His voice sounds choked, but he recovers. "But then I try to find out about *you*, and, Jesus, I'm just trying to screw you? What the hell is that all about?"

My cheeks are flushed and hot. "That's not what . . ." But I can't lie.

"Yes, it was," he says slowly.

I hate her. My mom. For making this so complicated. For making my life, my choices, this moment, about her. For rising from the dead at the worst times.

"Still, I wasn't trying anything."

I look at Paulo and nod.

"Do you want me to go?" he asks.

If I say no, it's not the same thing, I tell myself. *It's not begging him to stay. It's not being Ruby.*

I shake my head.

He comes over. He looks at me like he's trying to figure something out and then takes my hand. "Come on," he says, and we head back to the kitchen.

We sit at the table. I feel embarrassed for thinking the worst of him.

"I have posters up in my room, Dani. Old pictures. You could walk in and figure out things about me. But you don't reveal anything."

He rubs the back of his neck.

"I'm sorry," I tell him. "I didn't think." I stumble over the words and none seem right, so we sit in a silence that threatens to suffocate us.

"I'm nowhere near that smooth, anyway," he says. He smiles, and I know he's trying to make things better. But I feel like I've messed something up. I feel like a part of me I didn't even know was there suddenly showed up, a part I don't understand. I feel like something has changed.

After a while, he reaches over, taps the lotería game. He gave it to me as a souvenir from our trip to Mexico and I'd left it on the table. He pulls the box toward us.

"So like I told you the other day," he says, breaking the tension, "this is basically Mexican bingo, with pictures instead of numbers. I never really played it the way you're supposed to, because it's always been just me and my abuela, and when she used to work at the store a lot, it was basically just me." I imagine Paulo in the trailer, long days alone. "Usually I'd just look at the pictures."

He shuffles the deck. "I'd pretend they were sort of like signs for something. I'd pick a few cards and try to figure out what they were telling me."

"Were they ever right?"

"Nah . . ." He looks at the cards, and I think he's not totally convinced. "Here, pick some."

"Why?"

"Just pick a few. Pick six. That'll tell me something about you."

"You first."

He shrugs. "Okay."

He starts going through the cards and I watch him look at each one before making a choice.

Finally he puts six cards on the table between us.

"Okay," he says, holding up a card with a skull. "This one is because of la muerte, which took my parents." He tosses the card on the table and picks up one with a red devil on it. "And this one is because of the way they died." He studies the card. "He had something to do with it."

I don't know what to say, but Paulo just moves on.

"This is because of the blood that runs through my veins, my father's blood," he says, holding up a card with the Mexican flag on it. "And this one," he says, holding up a card with a flowerpot full of red roses on it, "is for my mother. She loved roses. Red, red roses." He looks at the card and kisses it before putting it down. "This one," he says, looking at the next card, one of a man carrying a guitar, "is because my father loved music. Couldn't sing a note and only knew three chords, but somehow it sounded just right, you know." He stares at the card and a look of sadness comes down like a veil over his face.

He picks up the last card, of a man holding a machete. "And finally, this is because . . ." He smiles, looks embarrassed. "This is one I always thought would be me. The man I want to be."

I look at the card. "You want to carry a machete?"

He laughs. "No," he says. "El valiente. It means 'the brave one.' Courageous."

Paulo looks at the cards and then at me. "Your turn," he says. He hands me the deck and I take it. I'm scared of what I'll see. I'm almost certain the bear will appear on one of the cards.

Each one feels full of meaning, like I'm holding somebody's story or history or future in my hands. I look through the deck slowly, not really knowing if I'll choose any card, but then some of the images make my heart pound faster and my hands tingle. I could easily pick out any six cards and lie about them. I could do that.

But I don't.

I pull out a card with a heart.

Then a sun. And one with a star.

A liquor bottle. And a woman.

Atlas.

I lay them out on the table, beneath Paulo's cards.

"This last one," I say, my voice suddenly shaky, "is how I feel, how I've felt as long as I can remember." I hold up the card with Atlas, the man carrying the world. Then I put down that card and pick up the one with the woman wearing a red hat, red shirt, red lipstick, and a short skirt that reveals her thighs. "Mostly because of this one, my mother. . . ." I look at the woman, who has a small, knowing smile on her lips. "She liked attention" is what I say to Paulo. "Lots of attention . . . but not from me." I put the card down before I think about it too much and pick up the next one.

I hold up the card with the star, trying to find the words for why I picked it. "This reminds me of her because it's a pinhole of brightness in a dark sky," I tell Paulo while looking at the card. "And there was something, I don't know what or why, that made me . . ." *love her . . . wish she loved me?* ". . . that made me love her, even though . . ." *even though I shouldn't have? Or I didn't want to? Was she right? Was I just a terrible daughter?* ". . . even though she made it hard."

I swallow and pick up the card with the sun. "But usually . . . usually she felt more like this." I look at the burning, consuming sun. This is how she felt to me. I couldn't get close to her. She never wanted me close to her.

I put down the sun and pick up the liquor bottle.

"This one," I tell him, "is because it's how I knew her best. With this in her blood. I always wondered what she would have been like without it . . . but now I don't know if I really want to know."

I put down the bottle card and pick up the one with the heart. With its thin veins and thick valves, I can almost hear it beating, almost see it pulsing. "And this one," I say, turning the card in my hand, tracing the outline of it as I try to find the words to explain. "This one is because . . . I want to feel empty and dull. But coming here makes something keep squeezing this." I point at the heart. "And making it throb and making it . . ."

I look at Paulo. His eyes are soft. "Making it hurt?"

I nod. I can feel it now, my heart racing. Each violent beat makes it feel bruised and swollen in my chest. I think my heart must be black and blue. I imagine it, a mottled thing in my chest, poisoning my blood, pumping that poisoned blood throughout my body.

Paulo reaches over and wipes away tears I didn't mean to cry.

I look at the scattering of cards and I look at Paulo and I want to ask him if we'll be okay. But I kiss him instead. Because I want to. Because I won't let her ruin this. I kiss him and pull him toward the couch and even though I can feel his hesitation, he follows me. And we kiss until my lips feel raw, and I pull him close to me and try to take away his past and he kisses me back and tries to take away mine. I never want to stop.

The room darkens, and I think the clock moves faster. Night falls and we're in the dark, on the floor, breathing fast, staring at the never-ending ceiling because something keeps us from going any further. We stay that way in silence.

Then Paulo reaches for my hand, holds it softly in his, and asks me if I want to hear the rest of his story.

Yes, I tell him, because his voice, the way he holds my hand, tells me he needs to. And I remember suddenly what he said at the Pink Store about his heart.

In the dark I can hear his breath. I can hear how it quickens. I think I can hear his heart, thumping faster as he starts talking. He tells me how on the day his parents died, the day a stranger came for them, he was eight years old. He was in his room. And when he heard the gunshots, he hid under his bed.

His movie flickers into my mind. I see the woman look toward an opened door and I picture myself walking down the hall, to a room with a bed pushed against the wall. I look under it, see a boy pressing his small face against the cold cement floor, staring out at the room so intently for so long, he can describe the exact shade of blue painted on the opposite wall. I can see it. *Those walls swelled, like they were breathing, and I heard the sound of water before the world became so, so silent, before a great bird came down and carried me away.*

The whole thing plays and replays like a movie in his head, he says. It makes me think of how our minds work and how grandmothers get strange feelings that send them flying across borders, swooping down to carry a little boy away, to safety.

Paulo says his heart turned to a black stone when he caught sight of them, his parents' bodies on the floor as his grandmother carried him away, and he says he died right there, in her arms, turned into a zombie who didn't wake until she helped him grow a new heart.

I squeeze his hand, bring it to my face, wish I could take away every bad thing that's ever happened to him.

I've made myself remember them other ways, too. The way they looked when they were smiling at me, or wearing a particular shirt or skirt. But the thing that bothers me is that's how I always remember them first. And I can't hear them anymore, he says. *I can't remember their voices. I can't remember the exact sound of my father's singing. And the harder I try, the quieter they get.*

He asks me if I remember my mother's voice, and I close my eyes and try. But it's like remembering a song; I know what it sounds like, but I can't truly hear it. It's just a memory, blurry around the edges, fading notes, becoming thinner, fainter.

All I can hear is a low, faint rumble. And it grows. Louder. Closer.

And I know it's the bear. Coming after me.

I can hear him running toward me. Finding his way back every time I banish him. I look out the window, waiting to see his face pressed against the glass.

I hear myself tell Paulo suddenly, "There's a bear coming for me."

He doesn't say anything and I wonder if he's heard me, but then he says, "What does he want?"

"He wanted my mother. He killed her." My voice doesn't sound like mine. I feel like I'm outside myself. "A wild bear, in our backyard. He mauled her and chewed her pinkies. But I know," I tell Paulo, "I know he was chasing her before then. And he finally found her and . . ."

I start laughing because the thought that flashes in my mind is *A bear ate my mother.* And it's like the dancing jackrabbit and Doña Soledad with her Joker smile. And then I'm thinking of Little Red Riding

Hood and how her grandmother was eaten by a wolf but a lumberjack killed the animal and opened him up and Grandma emerged from the belly alive and whole. And even if I found a lumberjack, even if I resurrected the bear they say is dead, even if we opened him up and Mom was there, I don't know that she would come out. I think she'd still stare back at me with that look on her face that said *Why are you bothering me?*

I would tell Paulo this, except I'm laughing and I can't stop. And the laughter turns to crying. I put my hands over my mouth and hear strange, high-pitched sounds coming from my chest, a screeching whistle, a signal for the bear.

Paulo puts his arms around me so tight I think I'll stop breathing and tells me I'll be okay, keeps telling me that, even though I don't believe him. Even though I'm sure my heart hasn't turned to stone but has exploded instead and the shrapnel is shooting and ricocheting around inside of me, piercing me.

We stay that way, until I'm too tired. Until nothing matters. The darkness becomes a thick blanket that muffles time and makes me sway between reality and sleep. *If I could stay here it wouldn't be so bad*, I think.

I have to go, I hear eventually. And I don't know if it's Paulo or my mother speaking, but there is a kiss on my cheek and a soft touch. And it doesn't matter because everyone goes. And my brain flutters with images of death and cards and the sun and voiceless words find their way into my ears and into my brain.

I've been here forever,
forever in the burning sun,
in the endless orange dust.
Something inside me is breaking,
or waking!

I'm almost asleep when those words jolt me awake and I look out the window.

He's there.

My breath comes quicker as I see him getting up on his hind legs, pressing his paws against the glass, opening his great mouth. I try to stay calm. I know this time he won't leave unless I face him. I have to follow him, wherever it is he leads me.

I get up in that darkness. And I walk outside to the barn, that tomb that holds the trailer. He walks ahead of me, but I can hear his breath in my ears the whole way.

Clocks spin,
nights rise,
days fall,
and I go back,
back,
back.
I'm unborn.

NEW MEXICO, 1992

As told by Shelly Falls

"Get the hell up," I tell Anna, hitting the lump on the bench that serves as seating in the kitchen area of our tiny trailer. A motor home, actually. A dirty motor home that our father drove from Colorado to New Mexico when I was two and my sister Anna Ruby was one, and planted out here in the middle of nowhere. In the middle of the desert.

If it weren't for him, we'd never know it was stolen. We'd never even know we once lived in Colorado. But he liked to tell the story of how he stuck it to the dealership where he'd worked. How he snuck into the place in the middle of the night and drove the motor home right off the lot with the keys he'd swiped earlier that day.

Picked you all up at the motel and we were a full eight hours away before the first salesman arrived and began to realize anything was missing.

He'd laugh telling us how he pulled one over on them. *They fucking owed me,* he'd say, *all that time fighting in Vietnam and I come back and I'm a salesman. Nobody even knows or cares about that war we fought. Nobody gives a shit. Well, fuck everyone. I gotta watch out for me. Gotta put a roof over your heads, food in my babies' bellies.*

There were plenty of times there was no food in our bellies, and when I ask Mama about where we lived, if it was a house and if we had our own room, she says we were nomads. That the road was our home.

"The road and motel rooms?" I ask.

She pretends she doesn't hear me.

I don't remember the long drive out here. My memories have always been full of dirt and the thick, stagnant, angry air of our motor home. Colorado has never been real to me. I don't believe it even exists.

"Get up!" I tell Anna Ruby again. She doesn't move. I kick her and she makes a sound like a whimper before thrashing her legs and nearly nailing me in the face with her feet. I shove her legs away, hard. "You're so useless!" I yell. The words escape my mouth and even as they're coming out, I think, *Stop! You sound just like him.*

She doesn't answer.

Mama is outside. I look out at her from the small,

dirty window of our trailer. Yesterday morning she was standing out there that same way, like the world had crushed her, while Daddy slept on the bed. Yesterday morning was when I woke up with bruises and a headache so deep it felt like my head would break. The first thing I remembered was how he'd choked me and hit me the night before because he knew I hated him and he couldn't do anything about it.

Mama holds a mug of coffee in one hand as she stares at the mountains. She looks tired. And old. And defeated.

She doesn't look like a woman who just killed a man.

She stands by the fence in her blue nightgown. I check to make sure it's really her even though I know it is. She looks so strange.

I sit back on the bench and think.

What the hell do I do?

I get back up.

"Let's go," I tell Anna Ruby. "Come on, we're going to school." I pull the brown blanket off her and she thrashes again like a wild animal. The look she shoots my way reminds me of the feral cats that roam the desert and I almost expect her to claw at my face, but she just snatches the blanket back and hides under it.

"I went yesterday and we'll both go today," I tell her. "We have to go!"

It's crazy! It's unreal. This isn't fucking real, I say to myself while I stare at Anna and try to keep my voice steady.

She doesn't move or say anything. I pull the blanket off her and throw it on the floor. She begins to thrash again and it pisses me off so I throw myself on her, ignoring the shooting pain throughout my body, and hold her down with my body. She shakes her head and I grab her face harshly, hold it in my hands.

"Open your eyes!" I tell her through clenched teeth. "Anna, open your goddamn eyes!" I push myself against her even harder.

This time she does, and I look into them, trying to connect with something. "Listen to me," I tell her. "We're going to school." I say the words slowly so she will understand. "We are going to get dressed. We are going to walk to the bus stop. And we are fucking going to school."

"I can't," she whispers. She tries shaking her head, but I have a tight hold on her face and she whimpers. I hold on tighter.

"You can," I tell her. "You will. We will. You don't have to pay attention. You can even say you feel sick. I don't give a crap. But you *will* go." I make a mental note that I will have to act extra normal. That I will have to make sure to laugh with friends. That I will be normal enough for both of us.

She stares at me and I go on. "If we don't go today, we won't go tomorrow. If we don't go today and tomorrow, the both of us, it will leave a trail. It will seem odd."

"We miss all the time. It won't matter," she says.

"It will matter this time." I slowly let go of her face. She turns away from me and lets out a deep sigh. I get off her and she carefully sits up, her feet on the floor. "Okay?" I ask.

She gives me a dirty look, but nods.

I turn away for a moment and out of the corner of my eye see her snatch the brown blanket and wrap herself in it again.

"Goddamn it!" I say as I reach for her feet and pull hard, drag her off the bench so fast her head hits the edge as she slides off.

"Damn you!" she yells, rubbing her head and whimpering again. "What the hell is wrong with you?" But she gets to her feet and looks at me.

I open the bench, grab her clothes, and throw them at her. Then I grab my own clothes and slam the bench shut.

"Get dressed!" I tell her. She stares at the clothes. "Now." Inside, I am seething. Inside, I am bubbling. But I try to speak to her in a steady voice. "We have ten minutes." I begin changing out of yesterday's clothes and into a pair of jeans, a long-sleeved shirt. Anna picks up her clothes and complies. I watch as she pulls on her boots. At the last minute, she carefully ties a black bandanna around her forehead. It makes her look like Daddy and I want to rip it off and ask her what the hell is wrong with her, but I say nothing and keep my hands at my sides.

Neither of us looks toward the end of the trailer, past the bathroom, to the foot of Mama and Daddy's bed.

We don't look at the lump on the floor covered by the quilt adorned with tiny red roses. We don't brush our teeth. We don't go near the bathroom. We pretend he's not there.

I pull on the ends of my sleeves, hold tight to them, making sure I don't forget. I wear my hair down, brushing it forward so it covers my neck, reminding myself not to flip it back for anything in the world. I make a mental note: No matter how hot it gets, *leave your sleeves down, keep your hair down.*

"Come on." I throw Anna her backpack and carefully pull my own over my aching shoulders.

I ignore the pain in my back, where the edge of the table dug in when he slammed me into it.

I ignore all the pain, in my legs, in my arms, in my neck. Then I open the door to our trailer and step into the glaring sun of the New Mexico desert.

I pull Anna by the hand.

Mama watches us as we walk around the junk littered in front of our motor home and out into the big open space that surrounds us. We're just far enough from the cluster of real mobile homes and trailers that we go mostly forgotten. And just close enough to keep us from being completely out in the middle of nowhere by ourselves.

"Going to school!" I yell at her.

She stares at us like she hardly knows us.

Her hair is hanging around her face. I look again, making sure it's her.

I see her hands, pale and white, grip her coffee mug, and then I turn away and Anna and I continue in silence.

But the image of Mama's hands stays with me. It fills my thoughts as we walk. I think about the unforeseeable strength of those pale, white hands. I imagine how they must have latched on to Daddy's belt and gotten it around his neck. How they must have pulled tighter and tighter, bringing him to his knees. They must have been locked in place, like a dog's jaw, unable to be pried open, unable to let go.

I don't know exactly, because it happened while I was at school. Anna stayed home because she was Daddy's favorite and she thought he would stay calmer with her there. *Maybe he won't hurt Mama with me here*, Anna said. We both knew it was a stupid notion, buy maybe he wouldn't kill Mama with Anna there. So I went to school. And Anna stayed.

And Daddy didn't kill Mama. But she killed him. I came home to Mama staring at the lump and Anna crying so hard she couldn't tell me anything.

Images of Mama's hands placing food in front of me, touching my hair, wiping my face, float around the darker image.

The sun pulses brighter, pulls me out of my

thoughts. Other homes come into view, but I'm scared to look around, afraid to see faces peering out of windows, faces that might know what has happened. Especially when we pass Doña Marcela's trailer. So I keep my eyes straight ahead, counting my steps to the small park where the bus picks us up. I focus on the rusty swing set, the monkey bars, the water fountain that barely trickles water.

"Just act normal," I tell Anna as we approach the others waiting at the bus stop.

Jalisa, Sammy, and Noel look at us as we come nearer.

"Hey, Rambo!" Jalisa yells at Anna, and then claps her hands as she laughs. "We missed you yesterday. What up, Rambo! Hey! I said hey!" She tries to get Anna to respond, but Anna just stands there, a glazed look on her face. "What the hell is up with you?" Jalisa says.

I try to shoot Anna a warning look, but she won't look my way.

"Don't worry about her," I tell Jalisa.

Jalisa is the youngest of us, but nothing fazes her. "Fine, be that way, looking like Rambo and shit and acting like you're too good to talk to me today."

"Leave her alone," I say.

Jalisa gives me a dirty look. "You ordering me to leave her alone?" She mimics me like I'm some kind of drill sergeant.

I feel my blood pulsing with anger. I want to punch

Jalisa in the face, see her body hit the ground, and again I think, *I'm just like him.*

Anna doesn't react to any of it, so I take a deep breath and try to keep it together like it's no big deal. Like everything is totally fine.

"What the hell *is* up with her anyway?" Sammy asks, looking at Anna. "You stoned or something?" He stares at her and when she doesn't respond, he shrugs and gives up.

I look at her, so far away that I wonder where she went. I have a horrible image of Anna breaking down in the middle of class and being sent to the office, where she will spill her guts to some stupid counselor. *Stay*, I say to her silently, hoping that she will receive my message telepathically. *Stay, damn it, Anna. Stay and help me with this.*

Inside, I sound desperate.

I focus on the frayed ends of my backpack strap and pull at them.

"Forget her, she's just being dramatic."

"I'm just tired," I hear Anna say suddenly, and a small surge of relief goes through my body. The corners of her mouth twitch, but her eyes look strange and dull. "Couldn't sleep last night."

"Oh yeah?" Jalisa says. "You know what works good for that? Beer. Just sneak a bottle. I know your daddy's got plenty." She puts an imaginary beer bottle to her mouth, throws her head back, and then looks at Anna. "Works like a charm."

"How the hell do you know?" Noel says.

Jalisa shakes her head. "Shut up," she tells him.

Anna sits down on the pavement and puts her face on her knees, hugging them close to her body.

I start counting the frayed threads of my backpack straps and try not to think. But the images come, faster than I can replace them with numbers or thoughts of something else. Anything else.

Her hands.

The belt.

Three four five

The gargling sounds he must have made.

Six seven eight

The way he threw me around that trailer. With hate.

Nine ten eleven

Anna's face when we looked under the quilt.

My voice that didn't sound like my own because it sounded too calm.

It's okay, Mama. . . .

Twelve thirteen fourteen fifteen sixteen seventeen eighteen nineteen twenty

I stop counting.

Jalisa is still running her mouth, but she's talking to Sammy. She likes him. I focus on the swings. The water fountain. The way the water dribbles out.

I touch my neck. Noel looks at me. I pull my hair forward. I hear the bus and see it in the distance, sending up dirt. *We're always covered with dirt*, I think. *We are filthy.*

The dust makes me think of smoke signals, of people lost. And I think, *SOS!*

But who would save us?

The bus comes rumbling up. Everyone gets on, except Anna, who doesn't even stand. I pull her up and push her, urge her. "Come on," I tell her. "Unless you want to go back and stay in that trailer all day . . ."

She glances back at me, that wild look again. She didn't think of that.

But I did.

I shove Anna into a seat and sit down next to her. The bus jostles forward again. I look over at Anna and nod, trying to reassure her, even as my own mind fills with thoughts of what we will do. *What will we do?*

• • •

I see Anna after third period, in the hall. People are shoving her out of the way as she stops every few steps for no reason than to look around, as if reminding herself where she is.

You are here, I tell her, *with me.*

"You okay?" I ask her when she finally gets to the locker we share.

She seems surprised to see me. "Are you all right?" I ask again.

She nods. "Yeah, sure."

I look around, whisper, "Have any of your teachers asked you anything? Has anyone looked at you funny."

She blinks. "What?"

"Damn it, Anna." I look at her, the way she's blinking. She reminds me of the soldiers in Vietnam that Daddy had always told us about since we were little.

Sometimes you'd see the poor bastards running, carrying their arms, literally carrying their own fucking arms. Or trying to run and then falling over, not realizing one of their legs just got blown the hell off. Other times, only their boots were left smoking on the ground, bits of their legs still in them. How would you like that? Huh? How'd you like coming across that, Shelly?

Then he'd laugh like he just told us the best joke.

It was the fucking apocalypse! he'd say before taking another swig of beer.

Anna's eyes fall on my bruised neck. I pull my hair forward even though it's already covering it as much as possible.

"Just a few more classes, okay? Just act normal. Can you do that?" She hasn't taken her eyes off my neck and I grab her chin and force her to look at me. "Anna?"

"What?" she says. I search her eyes and they finally settle down.

"Can you do that?"

She pulls away. "Yeah, okay. Fine," she says, even though I don't think she knows what I asked.

The bell rings and we go in opposite directions. I

offer a nod to my teacher as I slip past her just as the late bell rings, and she closes the door behind me.

"Turn in your homework from last night!" she yells as we settle into our seats.

And class goes on like always. I remind myself to raise my hand, to answer questions in a way that is neither too eager nor too disinterested. I force myself to joke with Aaron, who sits next to me. And laugh.

The bell rings. Three more classes.

Two.

One.

I stand by our locker, waiting for Anna to show up, but it's Joe who comes over to me instead.

"What the hell is up with your sister?" he asks. I had forgotten about Joe.

"I don't know what you mean," I tell him as I open the locker, blocking him from my view.

Joe. Fucking Joe. Always trying to save Anna.

He pushes the locker closed again and stares at me. "You girls are a sweet duo, aren't you?" He smiles, the way guys smile when they're sure you can't pick up on their shitty meanings. But I could. God, I knew how guys could be, how they were sure they were stronger, better, superior.

"If you don't like it, then quit coming around," I mutter.

He sighs. "Come on. All right, I'm sorry. I'm just wondering what's up with her is all. She's being . . ." He shakes his head. "I don't know, *weird*."

I pull my hair forward again and shrug. "It's nothing. Just our dad," I say, acting like it's no big deal.

There was no way to completely conceal from Joe what happened in our trailer, not after he and Anna have been dating for six months. Especially with Anna always running to him like he could save her.

The first time Joe dropped her off at our place, our dad was yelling so loud you could hear every filthy word he shouted at Mama. I remember sitting on the small steps outside our trailer, wondering where Anna was and why she hadn't been on the bus. I remember being scared or pissed or relieved when I thought, *Maybe you ran away. Maybe you hopped on a bus and got out, as far away from here as possible, like you'd tell me you were going to do when we were lying in bed at night and things were really bad. I could almost see you on that bus, getting farther and farther away from me. And I couldn't decide if I loved you or hated you for doing it. Because even then, I knew you would.*

But then I saw Joe's blue Mustang appear in the distance, barreling toward me, and coming to a stop just a few yards from where I sat. Anna opened the door, and I thought, *Stupid girl,* letting a guy bring her home. It was almost a good thing Daddy was too busy yelling or hitting or belittling Mama. I walked over to them and started talking loudly and pulling Anna out of the car, trying to make enough of a commotion so Joe wouldn't hear the words coming through the thin trailer walls. So he couldn't hear the man who loved us. Who hated us.

But Joe heard and he made out enough, and he looked at us with a kind of confirmation and pity that made me sick.

Yeah, Joe knew all our secrets. Or almost all.

I pull a few books from my locker and put them into my backpack.

He stands there and eyes me. "Are you guys, you know, okay?"

"Yeah," I tell him. "He took off last night."

"Really? Well, that's not really a bad thing, right?"

I shrug. *It wasn't, was it?*

Except it was. A very bad thing.

"Anything I can do?"

I almost laugh. Is there anything *he* can do?

Yeah, I think, *stop rubbing your fucking wealth and upbringing in our faces and leave Anna alone.* "No thanks. It's no big deal." I look past him down the hall and see Anna walking toward us.

Joe follows my gaze and puts an arm around Anna's shoulder when she reaches us.

"Hey," he says softly. "Shelly told me. I'm sorry." He squeezes her toward him and kisses her cheek. She stares at me wide-eyed.

"Don't worry," I tell her. "I'm sure Daddy will come back soon enough. Or maybe he'll stay away for good this time. Who knows?" I keep my gaze steady with hers. *Keep your mouth shut! Don't tell him. Don't.*

Her lips quiver, but she nods. "Right," she whispers.

"Come on," Joe says. "I'll drive you guys home."

"We'll catch the bus," I say. "Too far for you to drive."

"It's okay." He doesn't live forty-five minutes away from school the way we do. He lives in an actual neighborhood, with sidewalks and paved streets. His parents have steady jobs. He already knows what college he'll be going to next year.

"It's not a problem. Come on, let's go," he says, ignoring me and grabbing Anna's hand. I see how she leans against him, how she clutches his hand like he might keep her from falling. He smiles at her.

"I said we don't need a ride." My voice is tight, unnatural. The anger and jealousy I've kept in check all day slip out.

"Jesus, relax." Joe shakes his head. "It's no big deal. I mean, I got nothing to do and I already know where you guys live," he says quietly, the way people do when talking about something shameful. "It's the least I can do."

So you can feel like a hero, I think. And I hate him. And I hate Anna.

I shake my head, but he's already turned around with her. She doesn't look back at all. And I think, *You'll never look back! And I want to run over and shake you. I want to tell you something is happening to us. I think we're dying, Anna! That's what it feels like. And I want to save you, but I can't, because I don't even know how to save myself.*

Because I don't know how not to be angry, not to be full of hate, not to want to tear apart everything and everyone I'm supposed to love. And I hate that Anna lets everyone slip into her heart and I don't even have one. I hate that she never has to be the one who thinks, who remembers, who realizes that if Daddy is missing, his car should be too, but Joe will see it if he drops us off.

I stand there trying to think of an excuse or a way to stop Joe and Anna, and each second I think, they get farther away, and each second that passes is one less to get to the bus.

"Wait," I call out. They keep walking, Anna leaning on Joe like that, not looking back. I just need a minute to figure it all out. I just need her to stay.

"Wait . . . ," I say again. But she doesn't. They don't. They just keep walking.

• • •

We pass different neighborhoods, the houses farther apart and more run-down the farther we get from school. Then they disappear altogether and only mountains and dirt and dried weeds and barely blue sky surround us.

When we pull up to our trailer, I see Mama just where we left her. I notice she is barefoot, standing in the sharp pebbles and dirt. I see Daddy's car parked where it always is, by the side of the house, for anyone and everyone to see. It feels like a beacon, as inconspicuous as a damn disco ball. I notice the way Joe slows down, scans everything, takes it all in slowly, his eyes lingering on Daddy's car and then on Mama.

"Looks like he's back," he says as he puts the car in park. Anna looks over at him but doesn't budge. Joe's car is a two-door, so I can't get out until she does, and so we both sit there, looking at Daddy's beat-up Monte Carlo.

"Want me to go in with you?" Joe asks Anna.

"Jesus Christ!" I say, shaking my head. "Are you insane?"

He looks back at me. "What is your problem?"

"I don't have time for this," I say, gathering my backpack and pulling on the seat to stir Anna.

"No, I mean it. What do you have against me? I'm trying to help."

"We don't need your help," I tell him. "We don't need anyone's help, and you should get out of here before he comes out and shoots you."

I can tell the thought makes Joe nervous, but he grabs Anna's hand and turns his gaze on her and says, "I'll go in there with you."

Anna shakes her head, but makes no move. Instead she looks down and I think she's going to cry.

"You don't have to go home," Joe says. "I've told you. I'll help you."

This time, I hit the back of the seat hard.

"Let's go, Anna," I tell her. "Mama's waiting for us."

I want Anna to remember Mama. To remind her that we can't leave her.

She stares at Mama and I see something in her expression that makes my stomach turn. I wonder if she won't suddenly beg Joe to *Drive, just drive!*

"Anna! I'm not gonna sit in this car all day," I tell her. It's hot, and driving with the windows down has left me sticky with dirt and sweat.

Anna pushes the door open. But Joe doesn't let go of her hand and she turns toward him, searching his eyes, taking refuge there. For a horrible moment I think she'll blurt out the truth. *He's dead. She killed him!* Instead she stays loyal and silent. And Joe eventually lets go and leans in to kiss her unbetraying mouth.

"I'll see you tomorrow, then," he whispers.

She nods and gets out.

I push the seat forward and do the same.

"You're welcome," Joe mumbles. "Hey, is your mom all right?" I look at him and I want to tell him I didn't ask him for a ride, that nobody asked for his help and I don't owe him any thanks. But it's not worth it. So I slam the door shut and stand next to Anna.

"Can you just go?" I tell him. The sun pricks at my skin and reminds me where we are, who we are, what has happened. Joe's stupid questions irritate and piss me off. "Get the hell out of here already!" My skin burns and my mind is blazing, so when he doesn't go, I kick his car.

He gives me a long look. The kind that makes my words and behavior echo.

"You're a cold bitch, you know that, Shelly?" he says, and he revs the engine, throws the car into drive, and speeds away.

"Why'd you do that?" Anna asks.

"Do what?"

"Make him leave. Why do you have to be like that? He could've—"

"He could've what?" I cut her off. "He's too fucking nosy! And he thinks he's so much better than us, like he can save us or something. Because he's got money and he doesn't live *here*"—I gesture around us—"fucking here, in the middle of nowhere. And are you stupid enough to think anyone can save us? That a guy can save *you*?"

I can see how my words wound her, but I don't care. I'm glad. Maybe it'll get through to her that she can't depend on anyone. That she's better off without a guy in her life. All she had to do was turn her face and look at Mama to see that. Or look at us. "Is that what you think, Anna? That Joe will fix everything?"

"He . . . he loves me. . . ."

"Loves you? Loves you!" I shake my head. "You're so stupid! He wants to get in your pants, is all, Anna. That's all he wants. Why else would he hang out with you?" My words are like the tip of a knife, nicking her face, neck, and arms. She looks at me like I'm horrible. But I can't stop myself.

Anna's eyes are blue, the exact same shade as mine. But in her face they look bluer somehow and express more than mine ever could. Right now they reveal the exact degree of hate she feels for me. But the truth is, Anna is beautiful. She can make angry men love her. She can make boys forget who they're supposed to be in love with. But she's too soft and easily broken and I have to tell her these things so she can be tougher.

If I had the time to explain, I'd tell her I'm sorry I have to be this way. But I don't. Because there's Mama to worry about.

"Go inside, Anna. I don't have time for this."

I walk over to Mama, half expecting her to have burned to a fine crisp, standing outside for so long. The mug is on the ground, beside her feet. I reach for her hand, wondering if she'll turn to dust and blow away. But no, she stays, her hand small and thin but solid in mine.

"Come on," I tell her. "It's time to go in."

"I killed him," she tells me. "I killed him."

"Mama . . ."

"I didn't mean to . . . but I did . . . I couldn't stop." She looks at me. "What have I done?" she whispers. Her hand shakes as she looks back at the trailer.

The way she talks scares me.

I look at her, her face darkened by the sun and dirt and wind. She looks older than she did this morning. Her hair is tangled around her face. I reach to smooth it, to touch her and make sure she's real, and it's then that I see a white truck appear beyond her, on the horizon, heading in our direction.

"Let's go inside," I tell her. But she stays where she is.

The truck comes closer and slows down. I see Doña Marcela's daughter, Rosa, with the guy who started picking her up at our bus stop last year. Within a month, she stopped coming to the bus stop altogether.

Rosa is looking at us. I can just barely make out her face in the darkness of the truck's interior, but she is peeking out at us, just like she did when we ran to Doña Marcela's house in the middle of the night and she cracked open her bedroom door.

The guy is handsome, but his mouth twists in a way that makes me think he might spit on us as they drive by.

We all look at each other, but nobody waves, nobody calls out a hello. I'm not even sure Mama notices them, and then they're gone.

"Well?" Anna calls from behind us. I forgot she was there. I forgot she existed. The heat and the sun make you forget, make you unsure of what is real and what is a mirage. Maybe that's why Mama has been standing here all day.

"Go inside," I tell Anna.

She shakes her head. "I can't." She walks away, in the direction of the bus stop.

I want to go after her, but I stay with Mama. We

don't move. The white truck drives back again, this time without Rosa, heading toward the border.

Only when she starts to sway on her feet, dehydrated, her eyes half-closed, telling me it was all a dream, am I able to get Mama inside.

It was a dream, she mumbles. *A terrible, terrible dream.*

• • •

I give Mama water. I see her coming back.

I look at him on the floor. A body.

It will start to smell soon. I know we have to do something about it.

But what I do is sit with Mama while she smokes. And what I do is remember everything he ever did to Mama. I remember every bruise on her body, every welt on her face, every black-and-blue eye swollen shut. I remember every choking sound I ever heard in the middle of the night, until the gagging sounds fill my head and leave room for nothing else.

But somehow his nice smiles and his sometimes-happy eyes flash through my head. Was that real? Maybe. And the feel of my hand in his when I was little, and his arms carrying me. Quickly, I send that Daddy away.

And I'm left with the one who was always around. The one who I finally pissed off enough to hit me and tell me he was not going to be judged by his daughter, the one who picked me up and threw me against the table. Who hit me harder with every blow I landed back on him. Who finally had enough of my shit and threw me to the floor and put his hands around my neck until all I saw were black dots.

I hate you. I hate you. I hate you, I tell that guy.

I hold on to that hate. I let it fill every inch of my body. I let it run wild in my veins so I can figure out how to do what we have to do.

And when I open my eyes and see dark setting in, I just hope I have enough hate to convince Mama.

I sit on the floor and look at her lighting another cigarette, waiting for her to say something. She smokes half of it before she speaks.

"It's wrong. . . . What I did was wrong. I didn't mean to, but . . . ," she says. "You all have to know that."

"I know, Mama," I whisper.

"I'm as bad as him now. Worse." She looks at me and then quickly away. "I'm gonna have to pay with the rest of my life."

She takes another drag and I see how the cigarette shakes between her lips. Her eyes fill up and she blinks away tears and takes a deep breath.

"I don't know what'll happen to you girls. Foster homes, I suppose. I don't know. I didn't . . . I didn't think it through. I should've just—"

"No, Mama," I tell her before she can finish. She thinks she should've just kept taking the punches, taking the slaps, let Daddy expel every bit of his anger on her, on her body. "You shouldn't have."

"I would have, though," she says. Her voice is strained and I see the way she tries to keep her emotions in check. A lifetime of trying to keep herself in check. "I could have. But I couldn't let you . . ." Her eyes fall on me and the tears come out anyway. "I couldn't let you take it. I told him, the day he touched you girls I'd kill him. I told him."

She covers her face and her crying is quiet, but it shakes her whole body and it kills me. It kills me the way she huddles and cries and tries to keep it all in. I think she'll never stop shaking. I think she'll never run out of tears.

Finally, her shaking slows to a quiver. She takes a deep breath, reaches a shaky hand for her cigarettes. She lights another one and inhales likes she's drawing strength from it and then she lets the smoke out in a long, slow trail.

"You'll drive me to the police station in the morning," she says suddenly.

She looks at the body. "Or tonight."

I answer her. At first, I'm not sure I've said what I said. But then I can feel the words in the air, silent, invisible words swirling around, waiting to be acknowledged.

I repeat them. I make them solid.

"Let's bury him," I say, looking at her. "Tonight. Let's bury him. We don't have to tell anyone." The plan

I'd been coming up with while I filled myself with hate and thoughts of how unfair it was he could still hurt us, hurt us forever, send Mama to prison and Anna and me to who knows where, comes out in alarming detail. "Nobody will question it. We'll say he left. Just like last time, when we thought he was gone. When we thought he wouldn't be back and you started working at the gas station. We were fine, until he came back. We'll be that way again. Only he won't come back. Not this time."

Mama's eyes are getting wider with every word that comes out. I should stop. I should stop talking so she doesn't look like the soldiers Daddy talked about, the ones carrying their own arms. So she doesn't look like she's not sure yet if she survived. If she's still breathing. But my words keep tumbling out.

"We can do this," I tell her. "We can."

I get up and sit next to her. I touch her split lip, her bruised arms. I touch her hair and think of how he slammed her head on the table while she tried to protect me. I think of how she told us to *Get outside, get outside!* And we did. And she took the rest of those blows. For me.

"It's not fair," I tell her. "It's not fair what will happen if . . ." I feel tears slide down my cheeks and neck, under the collar of my shirt. "You can't leave us," I whisper, feeling like I've already lost her. Like the little we do have, each other, has already been taken away. "It's not fair," I say again.

I'm crying harder even though I try not to. I don't

want to cry. I'm filled with rage and anger. I'm strong, too fucking strong for him to bring me down.

But I need Mama. She rescued me and I need to rescue her. So I wipe away my tears and assure her.

"We won't say anything," I repeat. "We'll tell anyone who asks that he ran off, went to California. Or Arizona. Or Mexico. That's what we'll say." I look at Mama, but she looks at me so sadly, I know she'll say it's impossible. I know she'll tell me we can't.

"No," she says as she pulls me closer, tighter, my arms aching with each squeeze and that word puncturing my heart, which I hadn't known was filling with hope.

"Mama, *please* . . . ," I cry. *"Please."*

"Don't," she whispers. "Don't say California. Or Mexico. Or any of those places." She speaks slowly so I hear every word. I keep my head on her chest for a moment, listening to her racing heart, feeling it. "We'll keep it simple."

I look up at her and I understand. I wipe my eyes, my nose, even though I'm crying harder. Even though I'm choking on relief.

She nods and shushes me, smooths back my hair, pulls me into her again. "We'll just say he left. And we don't know where the hell he went."

I nod. And I thank God. I thank God even as I worry about my soul.

· · ·

The last time he left was at the beginning of the school year. But he came back just like I knew he would. I spotted his car before Anna did. I spotted it because I looked for it every day. Because I didn't want to be taken by surprise. It was after school and we'd walked home from the bus stop.

I remember wondering if we'd find Mama dead when we walked into the trailer.

But Mama and Daddy were both at the small table, drinking coffee. Daddy clean-shaven and fresh, looking back at us with eyes so blue.

"There they are," he said as we walked in. He stared at us like he couldn't believe we were real. "Jesus, when'd these girls get so beautiful?" he said to Mama.

Mama smiled. "They've always been," she said.

He got up and pulled us both to him, in one great hug.

His hair was short and his clothes smelled like cigarettes and laundry detergent.

"Daddy?" Anna whispered as he pulled away and looked at us again.

"Don't look so surprised, for Christ's sake. Of course it's me," he said. "In the flesh, baby. All polished up and feeling brand-new. And I am."

He looked at Mama and she smiled again. And she sat there and looked at us like she believed him.

She looked like she *wanted* to believe him. Like she'd give anything in the world for it to be true.

He pulled out a bracelet for Anna, one that looked

like the sparkly one Mama had on her wrist, and then pulled one out for me. And Anna asked him where he'd gotten them and he talked about somewhere he'd been in California and about how he'd found Jesus and now he knew how to be right because Jesus was with him. And I looked at the crucifix that hung over our trailer door, where Jesus had always been, and wondered how Daddy didn't see him there. But Anna went from being terrified to downright joyous. I kept my eyes on Mama to see if she believed any of this. And Daddy kept his eyes on me.

"You're awfully quiet, Shelly," he said. I remember how he said it and how he smiled, but I wasn't as stupid as Anna. "Aren't you happy I'm back?"

No. "I'm just . . . surprised, is all," I told him.

"Surprised?" He nodded and I knew he wanted to stare me down, but Mama was watching and Anna was talking, so he stared for just a second, just long enough for me to see he wasn't stupid either, and then he smiled bigger, tighter. "Course you are, baby," he said in just that way, that way that let me know he was still who he had always been.

I looked at Mama and saw beneath her smile that said *Yes, he's brand-new* to the fear just beneath it. She was who she'd always been too.

When we went to the buffet an hour away to celebrate Daddy's homecoming, to celebrate *him,* Anna looked like she was five. She looked like she'd forgiven him everything because he smiled at her and they shared cotton candy. There wasn't a trace on her face of the questions that were burning inside me, like *Where the hell has he been?*

And has he stopped drinking?

And where is the woman he left with, the one who stared at us from the passenger seat and look bored even as Mama yelled after him that he couldn't *take all the money, not all the money! What am I supposed to do?*

And does he really think a fucking bracelet is going to make us forget? Just forget everything?

Does he really think we believe he's any different?

And why? Why the hell did he come back?

Anna didn't ask any of those questions, and Mama didn't either. I only thought them, but I swear, as he sat there eating, I swear he could read every single one of them as they flashed through my mind.

And he hated me for them.

· · ·

The first sign he was *really* back was when he made Mama quit her job. He never liked her to work. Said he alone could provide enough for his family. Then the empty beer bottles showed up, in a line behind the trailer. I saw them even though Mama and Anna pretended they didn't. I noticed that the fresh, clean smell he'd come back with, the smell he wanted us to believe was salvation and meeting Jesus, was gone. And once again the warm, sour scent of beer emanated from every pore of his body. I knew exactly who Daddy was. And who he wasn't. He couldn't fool me.

So when the bottles clanked against each other, fell, and rolled with the wind, I made it a point for him to see me looking after them. I wanted him to know.

"Get that look off your face, Shelly," he told me. His face was red and shining with grease and sweat. "You always have such a look on your face, you know that? And it's getting so goddamn old."

Mama had gone to pick up her last paycheck from the gas station and Daddy was fixing a lawn mower he'd found on the side of the road in town. He was banging around among all the useless material he'd collected over the years and hoarded in big piles in front of our trailer. Always making so much noise, making sure I knew he could throw anything he damn well pleased as hard as he wanted, till he broke it, even. All that banging made my mouth loose.

"Yeah, it is," I told him. "It's getting old as hell, Daddy." I knew I shouldn't have said it as soon as the words were out of my mouth, as soon as I turned to go inside, and prayed to God he wouldn't throw something at my head.

He came over so fast, pulled the door open before I even had a chance to close it, nearly taking my arm off. And he threw every insult at me, filled the trailer with them.

But they couldn't reach me; they didn't cut and they didn't mean a thing. I watched as he got red and raged and his lips formed more and more meaningless words. I watched, half expecting foam to trickle from the corners of his mouth, as he towered over me and I was in awe that none of it—*none* of it—could reach me.

But Anna was there and she flinched at each of his words. Even though they were meant for me, they pierced her like just-sharpened arrows.

And by the time he was done purging all his hate and anger, she looked tired and defeated.

"Why do you ruin everything?" she whispered when he went back outside and drove away. Maybe to get drunk. Maybe to find Mama and unleash more hate on her.

"Ignore him, Anna," I told her. "You have to learn to ignore him and never expect him to be any different. Don't let your guard down."

She shook her head. "You make him like this. You don't believe in him, so he doesn't change."

It was the most warped pile of crap I'd ever heard, and I lunged for her before I could think. I grabbed her arm and dug my fingers in so deep, so hard, I could feel the veins and tendons and bone.

"Don't you ever, ever blame me, Anna. It's him!" I told her.

She stared at me. "I hate you," she said. It wasn't the first time she'd said that to me, but it was starting to sound truer and truer.

"You wait," I told her. "It's going to be the same, same as always." She shook her head, refusing to believe me, telling me I was wrong. I didn't know how she could still believe anything could be different, but she did. And even though it was backward, I was glad that Daddy was going to prove her wrong and me right. I let go and told her, "You'll see."

• • •

Three days later, not even two weeks after he came back with shiny bracelets, we came home from school, opened the door, and there was Daddy with a gun pointed right at us.

"You were right, Shelly," he said as he stood there, Mama in a chair next to him. "I'm bad through and through."

"I never said that," I whispered, looking at Mama.

He laughed. "You did, baby. You've said it every single fucking time I looked at you. Like I'm some kind of idiot, some kind of loser!"

"It's okay. Don't worry," Mama said. And quick as anything, he turned and held the gun to the side of her head.

"Yeah, don't worry," he told Anna and me. "It's not like I'm so horrible that I'd kill your mama right in front of you. . . ." He pulled something on the gun and it clicked. And my guts fell to the floor and Anna sounded like she was taking her last breath.

"Would I?" he said, and looked at me. "Would I, Shelly?"

I couldn't speak, but I knew I had to. I watched as his finger squeezed the trigger, then loosened.

"Daddy," Anna said.

"I'm not talking to you, baby," he said, looking at her. "No, I'm talking to Shelly. I wouldn't, would I, Shelly?"

I shook my head.

"I can't hear you," he said.

"No, Daddy," I finally managed.

He nodded and took a swig from the beer bottle in his other hand. "That's right, Shelly. I wouldn't. Because I'm not that bad, am I?"

"No, Daddy," I said.

"I provide for you all . . . and I came back, didn't I? I've fought in wars, for God's sake!" He drank the rest of the beer, set the bottle on the table, and put the gun back to Mama's head. "No . . . I'm not that bad . . . or maybe I am?" He stared at Mama as he thought. "Just when I think I'm not, I wonder." He shook his head and looked at me with drunk eyes. "But if I did ever do anything that terrible, whose fault would it be, Shelly?"

I looked at Mama and I swear she shook her head a little, but I knew the answer he wanted and I gave it to him.

"It'd be my fault, Daddy."

"Whose, Shelly?"

"Mine, Daddy."

He pulled the gun away from Mama's head and looked at it. "Well, you remember that when you want to look at me with judgment. You just remember that when you think I'm so bad." He turned to me, desperate, and said, "If you would just believe in me, sweetheart, if you just would," and for a moment, I saw in him whatever it was that Mama and Anna loved in him and I hated that he could do that.

"Yes, Daddy," I said.

And he put the gun in his waistband and stumbled outside. A moment later, we heard the roar of his car.

"I'm fine," Mama said as she reached a shaky hand for the cigarettes on the table. "Don't you worry, I'm just fine. He didn't mean any of it."

The next morning she made eggs and toast and he sat at the table and ran his hands over his face. "I was just foolin' yesterday, you all know that, right?" he said. "Just a stupid game. Gun had no bullets." He smiled like we were stupid little girls, like how could we ever believe it *had bullets!* "Your daddy just plays stupid games, that's all."

And Anna's eyes flickered with something like hope and faith and I stared down at my eggs to make sure he didn't see what flickered in mine. And just like that, things were the way they'd always been.

• • •

Mama and I do it before we can change our minds. Just the two of us, because Anna is who knows where and it's better that she's not here.

We grab some shovels Daddy keeps among all the junk outside. I wonder where he might have gotten them. I picture him spotting them in a dumpster and determining they were still good before grabbing them and throwing them into the backseat of his car, never imagining they'd be used to dig his grave.

We wait for the dark.

We don't worry about passing cars. Nobody passes through these parts at this hour. Not once when he had her pinned down, not once when we were little and called for help. People never see anything anyway. Even though they know everything.

We wait until it is pitch-black.

And then we start digging.

The scrape of the shovel sounds louder than a scream. And the digging is harder than I expected. It takes a lot longer. We spend hours making that deep, dark hole, disturbing the earth.

When our hands get raw and soft blisters erupt, I go inside for towels to wrap around the handles. On my way out, I see the crucifix hanging over the door and I close my eyes and walk past Jesus.

When I get back outside, Mama is muttering, but I can't make out anything she's saying. I hold a towel out to her, but she ignores it and keeps shoveling.

I think we've dug deep enough, but Mama says *Deeper*. At least three times, she says *Deeper*.

We have a small ladder in the hole with us now, a

rope tied to it so we can pull it out after. I look up at the sky from deep in that hole.

Smoky clouds rush over the moon. There are no stars to witness our sin. But the moon, the moon sees it all. And the sound of yipping coyotes in the distance makes me worry that the moon has dispatched some kind of wild vigilante justice for Daddy.

I shiver, worried the hole will cave in on the two of us and Anna will come back and Mama and I will be gone and she'll be left with Daddy's corpse.

"That's deep enough," I tell Mama.

"Deeper," she says, and I realize it will never be deep enough for Mama.

"That's enough, Mama," I tell her. "Enough."

She looks up at the moon and stays quiet for a long time before she says, "All right."

I climb the ladder propped on the side of the dirt wall, pull myself up and out. "Come on," I tell Mama as I look back down into the hole. Slowly, she pulls herself up and out.

We pull the rope and the ladder clatters up.

"Now," I tell her.

And we both know what's next. I look at the trailer, dark except for the dim night-light Anna and I have had since we were children. Always scared of the dark.

• • •

When I open the door, Mama stays silent. She walks to the end of the trailer, grabs one end of the blanket, and begins pulling with a strength I never guessed she had.

I watch.

There's a smell. I hold my breath and gag. I sway, then steady myself and go to help Mama.

She shakes her head. "No!" she says.

"Mama . . ."

"No," she repeats. She lets out a breath, grabs the blanket again. "Close your eyes, Shelly. For God's sake, close your eyes."

My knees are weak. My arms shake and I think it's because of all the shoveling, but I can't be sure. I fall on the bench and do what Mama tells me. And then, because I can hear her sliding the body along the floor, I put my hands over my ears.

I hold my breath until I feel dizzy. And I suddenly feel far away, and I'm glad.

The world is black and dreamy. I'm floating in my own head. I'm dizzy enough to not think about the terrible thing that has happened, that is happening.

I start dreaming of things that don't make sense. I start seeing the sun and Anna's face. I see the moon and the clouds from moments ago. I hear the yipping of the coyotes. Then I see Daddy.

I see his face.

And I remember.

My eyes snap open and I run, but Mama is already

at the edge of the hole in the ground and she is just now pushing him in.

There's a loud thump as he hits the bottom. I feel it in my chest, in my whole body. It shakes the earth.

I walk over and grab the shovel and start throwing dirt on top of him. We both do, and we don't stop, even though my arms feel like they will break and my back burns with pain. I keep going. Mama keeps going.

We keep going.

My heart is racing, my mind trying to understand the panic that comes and goes.

I try to calm down, but I can hardly breathe.

And then there is not enough air in the world and the shovel slips and I start crying and Mama is with me.

But I can't speak, not a word will come out, because I can't breathe.

I make animal sounds, horrible sounds that are barely sounds at all.

I feel Mama holding me. She's whispering words, but only the horrible hissing from within me registers.

I think of rattlesnakes, and I worry we are in a pit full of them. I worry Daddy has called them on us.

I can see Mama's face. *The dark will be gone soon,* I think as I look at the sky. *The sun will be out and will burn bright and we'll get caught. We have to finish.*

"I'm okay," I manage finally, through gasps and hiccups. "I'm fine." I get up and grab the shovel. "I'm fine," I tell her again, shoveling more dirt into the hole. "I'm fine."

It's all I can say, because I think my soul flew away. I'm just a body, like Daddy.

I swallow hard. And I wonder what I am. And Daddy's words haunt me.

I'm bad through and through.

• • •

When we're done, we shower. After we shower, we sit.

"I'm driving his car across the border," Mama says. I nod.

"I'll get a ride back somehow." She stares out the window. The sun is up. Another day has begun. Somehow. The sun is too bright. The kind of bright that makes your eyes pulse and your head hurt. Mama is dressed in jeans and a white thermal shirt, her hair semiwet. She looks like Mama, the same as always, except for that look in her eye. Like someone who hasn't slept but is somehow more alert, more aware of any sound or movement.

Moments later, we hear the sound of tires. Then the slam of a car door. Followed by another.

Something in my stomach lurches and Mama hurries to her feet.

"It was all *me*," Mama says quickly. "All of it was *me*, you understand?" She rushes to the window and then to the door, steps outside, closing it behind her.

"Hello," I hear her say. I get up and look out the window and see Doña Marcela with her daughter,

Rosa; Rosa's boyfriend; and Anna. They all stand close to Mama.

Doña Marcela is carrying something in her hands. I can tell from the way it's wrapped that it's a container of soup from Delia, the lady who runs the small kitchen in the gas station. Mama knows Delia from when she worked there. Doña Marcela hands the container to Mama and I can picture Delia in that turquoise shirt she always wore and with an apron around her waist, making soup. Wordless, because she spoke to no one. I can see her now, carelessly washing and chopping vegetables so the water splashes on the floor and bits of carrots fly up around her.

But the chicken, that she chopped with precision. If you listened carefully, you could hear the loud crack of bones, of bodies being broken in half, washed, and thrown into boiling water.

People wanted to believe Delia's soup cured every ailment, sickness, hangover, emotional strife. Her chicken soup made its way to houses where tragedy had struck.

To mothers who had lost children.

Women with two or three or more children whose husbands had left them.

Women who just killed their husbands.

Once I went around back to the gas station kitchen and saw Delia break a live chicken's neck.

Pluck its feathers.

Drain its blood.

That's what made the soup so good, people said. It was fresh.

I look at the soup in Mama's hands and remember the way Delia would wave at me with the knife in her hand when I'd come looking for Mama, making sure she was there and that Daddy hadn't come back and done something to her.

I rush to the bathroom and vomit. Wipe my mouth, then go outside.

Doña Marcela looks at me and I can tell she knows. I see the way her gaze makes its way over to Daddy's car and then the patch of dirt where we buried him.

"I thought I saw your husband leave," Doña Marcela says. "Last night."

Mama's face drains of the little color she has left and I think again of Delia and her knife and the chicken and I swallow back the fresh bit of vomit that comes up. Doña Marcela glances at the car and continues.

"Or maybe it's tonight I will see him leaving." She and Rosa's boyfriend exchange looks and he nods.

Mama watches them for a moment. "I . . . I . . ." She turns her head slightly in the direction of Daddy's car and I can see her struggling to understand exactly what Doña Marcela is saying.

"Tonight, I think he's leaving tonight."

Mama makes eye contact with Doña Marcela and says, "Yes, that's right. He's going . . . to find work. Not much he can get around here."

"No," Doña Marcela says. "Not around here. He's

got a bad reputation with everyone around here."
Mama keeps her eyes on the woman and then nods.

"You won't be alarmed, then, when you hear him take off in the middle of the night?"

Mama looks at the trio. "No, I won't. . . ."

Doña Marcela takes in the bruises and marks on Mama's face and neck. She gestures toward Anna. "She showed up at my door. Slept on the couch."

Mama looks down at the ground. I think she's hiding tears and I think we are all thinking of the night so long ago when we thought Daddy had gone completely crazy and we ran to Doña Marcela's house for safety. Mama nods, and then, without any more words, Doña Marcela, Rosa, and her boyfriend get in the truck and drive off.

Anna heads inside, but Mama watches them drive away. After a while she says, "We'll leave the keys in the car tonight." Then she sits down on one of the beat-up lawn chairs in Daddy's pile of junk and pulls out her cigarettes. I watch as she tries to regain control of her body but keeps trembling.

I go to check on Anna. She's sitting on the table, staring at the floor where his body was. Just stares at the spot. Then she gets up and pushes past me, opens the refrigerator, and takes out one of Daddy's beers. She looks at me as she opens it, takes a long gulp, and then wipes her mouth.

"Why'd you leave?" I ask. "Are you okay?"

"I went to hell," she says. She puts the beer back

in the fridge and slams the door shut. "To say hi to Daddy."

• • •

That night, I pull my bed out from under the bench and stare at the ceiling. Mama is sleeping, or not sleeping, in the front seat. I don't think she can hear Anna, or maybe she can and she hears Anna pray and hopes it will save us all. Or maybe Mama is praying too.

The room and bed at the end of the trailer are empty.

Anna prays quiet prayers that make her cry. And even though I want to tell her not to bother with prayers, I fix my gaze on the crucifix hanging over the trailer door.

Jesus looks so small and helpless. I used to pray to him until I realized I was praying to a man pinned to a cross, holes in his hands and ruined feet, gashes in his sides and a crown of thorns on his head, his agony evident from his face and the blood perpetually running from his wounds.

I felt guilty then, asking him for anything. Jesus had bigger problems. But I also thought he owed me. Because he was the Son of God and could make anything happen.

Why? I ask him now. I don't ask him for anything else. Just an answer. But he looks back at me with that sad look on his face and I feel a pang of guilt again.

And then I close my eyes and feel myself falling into sleep. But he's there looking at me, so I talk to him.

You remember that time, I ask him, *when he held his gun to her head? And when we were little and had to run to Doña Marcela's house?*

I was barefoot and the pebbles dug into my feet as we fled—Mama carrying Anna in her arms, and me blinking hard to see straight in the dark night.

The first trailer we came to was Doña Marcela's. The outside light flicked on and the door opened just before we got to it. We hurried up the wooden steps and into her small living room. She closed the door behind us and locked it, and Mama fell into a chair, Anna still in her arms. I stood next to her until Doña Marcela took my hand and led me to the couch. She didn't say anything, just continued into her kitchen, filling a teapot, getting a cup and saucer. She plucked leaves and twigs from a plastic bag and dropped them into the cup. Stood waiting for the water to boil and then poured it into the cup.

I watched her movements. Her hands looked as harsh and as soft as they'd felt when she held my hand. She made the tea and brought it over to Mama.

"Hierbabuena," she said. My mother looked up at her like she didn't know who Doña Marcela was, let alone why she was handing her a steaming cup.

"Drink this tea," Doña Marcela said. "Good herb."

Doña Marcela took Anna from Mama's arms and

put her on the couch. Then she went to a room in the back of the trailer where I saw her daughter, Rosa, poke her head out. Quickly, I walked over to Mama. I wanted her to hold me the way she'd held Anna, but she had the tea in her hands now, so instead I watched as she lifted the trembling cup to her dry lips. I touched her arm and her hair. I heard the shaky breath she took and the light clatter of the cup as she returned it to the saucer and the way she winced when the tea went down her throat. I stared at her neck, red and blotchy and already bruising.

"Why . . . ?" I asked her. She shook her head softly, but I had to ask. I wanted to know. "Why'd you ever marry him?"

She sucked in her breath, startled by my question. But she began telling me why. He was broken even before the war, she said. But she loved him and thought she could fix him.

Then one day, he's at my house, on one knee when I open the door. No ring in his hand, just a draft notice.

I try to picture it in my head. I try to see Daddy like that. But I can't.

He needed a reason, he said, a reason to come back. So I said yes, because . . . he looked so scared. Mama started to cry then and set the cup and saucer on the round table on her other side. *I thought I'd keep him together. But then he left. And he came back worse. And now . . .* She looked at me. Then at Anna. And put her face in her hands.

I looked at the tea she had set down. The light amber liquid looked pretty, like magic. I took the cup and lifted it to my own lips, sipped it carefully. It tasted like mint and lemon but also like dirt and trees. I didn't like it, but I liked the name. Hierbabuena. Good herb.

Doña Marcela returned with blankets. She covered Anna with one and handed another to Mama. Then I noticed a washcloth in her hand. She led me to the couch. When I sat down, she kneeled and wiped my bare feet with the warm washcloth.

I don't know why, but it made me cry. I held my hands over my face as the tears kept coming and Doña Marcela hummed and wiped gently. And I felt like something in me came undone.

When she finished, her hands guided me next to Anna, stupid Anna, who was already in a deep sleep. Who didn't even have to run. Who had been half-asleep and whining that she wanted her bed as Mama carried her. What would she remember of tonight? Maybe she wouldn't even know what had happened.

But as I lay there next to her, I knew I wouldn't forget. I wouldn't forget Mama's heavy breathing that filled the night, or the small whimpers that escaped her mouth as we ran and ran, or the pebbles that imprinted themselves on my feet forever.

I fell into the black hole of sleep, and even though Doña Marcela's humming penetrated the darkness, it couldn't cover up the sound of the whimpering and Mama's breathing. I knew then that's what people sounded like when they were scared, desperate. I knew then that we were all animals. Prey. I worried we would attract coyotes or other predators from their dark caves. I watched the door for as long as I could keep my eyes open.

In the morning, Mama was curled up on the small chair she'd been in the night before. She was still looking at me and Anna, and I wondered if she'd slept at all.

Doña Marcela gave Mama more good herb tea.

And then we got up and left. Out into the bright morning.

I looked down at my feet. They would get dirty again, but I followed Mama as she carried Anna and we walked the dirt road that led us back to our place.

When we walked in, Daddy was dressed and I had a flash of him as he'd been the night before, in just his underwear as he fell and crashed all over the place trying to grab Mama. How he finally caught her, climbed on top of her like that, nearly naked, and wrapped his thick hands around her neck. She'd tried to free herself; her face had turned colors. She'd looked like she would burst, and her tongue glistened as she tried to yell but only spit came out.

"Good morning," he said. And moments later, there was Mama again, standing by the sink with that weary smile.

I can still see his face now, through cigarette smoke, staring at me like he hated me because I knew what he was. I didn't care if he was broken before. I didn't care if he was scarred for life. I didn't care about anything but me.

And Mama.

And Anna.

You remember? I ask Jesus. I look at the door, think of the animals that can smell Daddy's body and will stampede in at any moment and find us.

They'll trample Mama.

They'll swallow Anna whole.

And me, maybe they'll just circle me forever.

Somewhere, I hear a loud roar.

· · ·

It's not the roar of the engine that wakes me. I hear it, but it's almost like a memory that has floated into my dream. What wakes me is Anna's ice-cold grip on my arm.

"Shelly!" she says. "Shelly!"

I look over and see Anna's eyes wide and scared. "He's back." Her whisper is so tight and high, it sounds like it could break. "He's back, he's come back for us, Shelly." She starts crying and my body fills with fear as she mutters things that don't make sense.

"He's back. . . ."

"Anna . . . he's never coming back," I whisper as I pull her close, hold her tight, try to explain about the car.

But she keeps on. She gets up, looks out the window, and when she can't see anything, she opens the door.

"He's back! He'll come after us," she says. "I know it."

I try to pull her inside, and Mama is next to us now and she's holding Anna and she's telling her everything is okay, but Anna pushes Mama away. She pushes me away.

"You're wrong!" she tells us, over and over, as she cries and finally lets us bring her inside.

"He'll come back for all of us!" she says. "Especially, *especially* for me. Because I was supposed to believe in him!"

I look at Mama, but she looks as scared and lost as I feel, as wild as Anna looks, and all she can do is hold and soothe her. But even as Anna quiets down, I keep hearing her repeat the same thing.

He'll come back for all of us. Especially, especially *for me.*

And I want to tell her it's not true, but I can't.

I can't lie to her.

Because I think she's right. I think he'll be back for all of us.

PART
THREE

Shelly heard me. Or she heard the bear. Because she found me in the trailer in the middle of the night.

Somehow she knew he'd come to show me the bench that served as my mom's bed when she was younger and that he'd opened the cabinets and pulled out clothes and sheets and pictures and other relics of their past. Somehow she knew he'd wrapped a black bandanna around my forehead and blocked the door so I couldn't get out.

"Anna," she said when she saw me. I hadn't heard her come in. I wanted to run past her, outside to the desert, keep running until only nothingness surrounded me. But all I could think was that she had come. She hadn't left me alone with the bear.

So when she kept staring at me, when she started crying and telling me about the life that happened in that trailer, I didn't run. I didn't leave her. Not when she'd come for me.

Now the sun is coming up and we are sitting here, exhausted from having purged and absorbed too much.

She looks over at me and I recognize for the first time those things I'd see when I looked at Mom. The secrets that were always there, locked somewhere deep inside, buried and pushed down, but now they have burst, exploded, landed around me.

Shelly leans back and closes her eyes, but keeps talking. "Your mom ran away a few weeks later. Never heard from her again. Joe told me some time later that he gave her money and a ride to the airport. He was going to go with her." Shelly smiles, but it disappears quickly. "She told him he could never love someone like her. That she wasn't good enough for him." Fresh tears slide out of Shelly's closed eyes.

My mind is still reeling from everything, everything I know now and what it all means, and I'm trying to keep it all straight in my head, even though my mind aches and feels soft.

"We kept thinking she'd come back," Shelly says, shaking her head. "Your grandmother died of lung cancer a couple of years ago. But every day she sat waiting and looking out at the desert, waiting for Anna to emerge." Shelly looks out the dirty trailer window like she might catch sight of my mom in the distance. "But she never did. And it was my fault she left. I couldn't help her."

She looks around the trailer. "I told Mama we

should go. But she wouldn't leave in case Anna came back. So I built that house with every cent I'd managed to save, so at least she wouldn't have to live in this trailer where so much happened. But when the house was finally finished, your grandmother couldn't bring herself to spend one night in it. She slept here. Every night."

Shelly looks like some kind of soldier on a battlefield. She looks like she needs medics to come and put her on a stretcher and carry her to safety. She reminds me of Mom, the way she looked tired so often. Tired because of all of this.

My eyes fill with tears and I whisper her full name. "Anna Ruby . . . ," I say. "Anna Ruby . . ."

"Your grandma read about some waterfalls in Georgia named Anna Ruby Falls. Said she was going to take us there one day. Anyway, I'd already been born when she read about them, so your mom got the name instead . . . Anna Ruby Falls. She was proud of it, always saying the whole thing whenever anyone asked her."

"Anna Ruby Falls . . . ," I say. I look at Shelly. "I didn't know. I didn't know her at all."

I always thought I knew her better than anyone, that I knew who she *really* was. I was her constant. I was a floating camera, watching her, judging her all the time. Watching the things she didn't care to hide from me, the way she dressed, the way she drank. The way she was quick to backhand me. She didn't have anyone else. She only had me. Only me. So I was the only one who could know, really know, who she was. I knew how terrible she was.

Except I didn't know anything.

"She never told you that story?"

I shake my head. "I . . . I didn't even know . . . her name was Anna. She just went by Ruby. Only Ruby."

Shelly looks at me and we sit in silence.

"I thought she was Ruby . . . ," I tell her.

I didn't know her at all.

• • •

We walk toward the house, squinting at the bright day.

I can see the bus from here, headed for school, and it looks more out of place and irrelevant than ever. I remember it was yesterday—*yesterday?*—I started school and watched Paulo's movie. I shake my head and almost cry at how time keeps floating around me, escaping me, sneaking up on me.

"I have school," I say aloud. "It's only the second day. . . ."

Shelly looks at me, a crease in her forehead. "Get some rest," she says.

When we get inside the house, she starts making coffee and I sit at the kitchen table wanting to ask her more questions but not knowing how. Not now.

She has to work tonight, she says, taking a sip of coffee and putting a cup down in front of me. She stares at me when she sees me touching the bandanna.

She looks worried, as if she regrets telling me anything. She sits and rubs her forehead.

I get up and I hug her and I whisper *I'm sorry I'm sorry I'm sorry* until she leads me to my room and tucks me into bed and smooths my hair and kisses my forehead.

She tells me there's nothing to be sorry for. She smiles at me, and I think it's the first time I've seen her smile.

And then she leaves.

My head is full of the past and present. Images and objects and people I know and don't know float in and out, surround me, and disappear again.

I wake up when the sun is going down, and get up because I can't go back to sleep. When I see the note on the counter in Shelly's handwriting telling me she's gone to work, dread and panic fill my chest. I'm alone in the house again. I can't stand the emptiness. I get dressed and go outside and stare at the setting sun. I beg it to come back, to burn me and my thoughts and a past I was never a part of but that feels like it could kill me.

The sun keeps falling, dipping down past the horizon, illuminating the sky in dusty pinks and delicate oranges devoid of anger and fire. *No*, it seems to say.

I walk anyway. I think about walking to Mexico. But my feet carry me in the opposite direction, to Doña Marcela's house. When she answers the door, she lets me inside and I sit down at the table.

The kettle screeches.

Moments later, she sets the tea in front of me and I look at it. The amber liquid.

Hierbabuena.

I drink it and ask her for another cup. I fill myself with it. I fill myself with good herb.

She gently tells me to lie down on the couch to rest and I do. When I close my eyes, I hear Shelly's words. I think of my mother on this couch where she once slept, in a place she once ran to for safety in the middle of the night. I bury my face in the cushions. And I smell earth and heat, salt and sky. And I think it's her.

I think it's you.

I breathe in deeply and choke on silent tears. Silent sobs.

And I cry myself to sleep.

• • •

I feel the pounding of the earth before I see the bear.

I feel the rumble beneath me. And I know he's coming.

But now I know everything.

Don't worry, I tell myself. Even though the pounding is getting stronger and my heart is beating in my throat. Even though my hands have gone cold.

No te preocupes, Paulo's grandmother says. I look

to the side and there she is, her hair flowing about her. And then she's ten feet away, twenty, and then perched on top of faraway mountains.

The earth shakes.

Rocks fall from the mountaintops and crumble to dust when they reach the bottom.

I stare at Doña Marcela, who floats above the mountains, watching.

I can't do it, I tell her. *I can't do it!* I scream.

She puts a finger to her mouth, shushing me. I can see her breath. It comes out in a great puff. It becomes clouds illuminated by the moon and stars.

I can already imagine the bear's paw over my face, the heaviness of it, the strength behind it. I can already feel him crushing my chest. I can already feel the scratches on my skin.

When a bear keeps coming for you, stalking you,
you must make yourself big,
you must make noise,
you must fight back.

I don't know where the voice comes from, but it fills my head. And I know instantly that I have to fight the bear. It's the only way he'll go away.

But I can't.

The earth shakes more violently and I fall to the ground. When I look up, I see Shelly close by, but she's on the ground too, and when I try to get to her, I see him.

Running.

Running.

His breath heavy, his mouth foaming.

Heading toward us.

I try not to think of his teeth and claws piercing my flesh. I try not to think of suffocating under the mass of him, his bristly fur. I close my eyes and wait.

But the earth stops shaking. And when I look again, I see he has stopped about a hundred yards from me. And he is waiting.

I look at Doña Marcela and she points to the sky.

The stars pulse like hot little diamonds. Thousands of them. Millions. And the clouds move like fog across the pale moon and then swirl and dance and transform. They become eyes, and face, and hair.

They become Ruby.

She floats down in front of the bear and I understand. She has come back. She has come back to help me fight the bear.

My chest swells with a million things I want to say. In seconds, it all comes out, without any words. And she smiles and I hear her. God, I hear all the things she wanted to say. And it breaks my heart even more because if I'd only known . . . if I'd only known, we might have had a chance.

She hasn't moved, yet I feel her all around me.

Remember this, I tell myself. *Remember all of this when you wake.*

I look at Shelly and she is crying, but she gets up and walks toward us.

The bear drags his paws on the dirt like a bull.

Seconds pass.

Infinity.

And then he charges.

His face changes as he gets closer. It transforms to faces I've seen before, the faces of men who spent nights in the backyard pool with my mother. They laugh, smile, stalk, but Mom just stands there.

The bear rears up on his hind legs, but Mom is everywhere. She is strong now, she doesn't even flinch.

He can't reach her. Even when he puts his paws out, so close to her head that her hair flutters, she just looks at him, like he will never get to her. But I know. I know he can. I know he has.

I scream. The stars turn red; they turn into a thousand hot little suns. I see pink water. I see Helen watching from a window. I see myself in my room.

She tried to fight him. But she wasn't strong enough. She lost.

Shelly screams and I'm back in the desert. She charges the bear, running and running and shaking the ground.

I yell, but she doesn't hear me. She collides with his massive body and a thousand sparks explode in the dark night.

She is thrown to the ground and the bear stands on his hind legs. I watch as he transforms into a flickering image of someone who looks both familiar and like a stranger. He has blue, blue eyes.

He sneers at my aunt and she is up on her feet again, charging again, clawing at him, tearing out patches of fur.

Mom watches.

Shelly keeps going. She punches and pounds the bear and he makes horrible noises. Yelps that echo through the desert. And this makes him step back, and another face flickers over the bear's. This one resembles Shelly.

I know it's my grandmother.

Shelly notices the face and stops. The bear looks at her and closes his eyes, and big tears flow down his face.

Shelly cries quietly. The bear reaches for her and pets her head and this makes her cry harder. And then he takes her in his arms and cradles her and whispers words I can't understand.

He takes her away, gently lays her on the ground far from us, and then turns and sets his eyes on me.

I feel Mom around me. I make myself bigger. I make a sound I don't even recognize as my voice as he charges. I brace myself for the blow.

But he doesn't charge at me. He stands there, his face flickering with so many images. Here's what I see:

My mother lying under a hot sun. The sun kissing her skin.

My memories of us together, that bear always lurking in the background.

The way her room looked at night, how the ceiling spun, how her memories made her dizzy.

Mom crying, and how, once, I touched her hot tears.

How I looked at her.

How she treated me, how she wished she could have been different.

How she tried to stay.

All the things Shelly told me happened.

He waits, until I see it all.

And I reach out my hand. I reach out to touch his prickly fur, but I feel nothing. I reach again, brush my hand against him, feel only air.

He walks away and with one, two, three strikes of his enormous paw, he makes a hole and stands at the edge and looks at me.

He's been following me for months. He's roared me to sleep and haunted me since the day I was born. He killed my mother.

But now I don't want him to go.

I race toward him, but he closes his eyes and falls,

and falls,

and falls.

I watch as he tumbles through the darkness.

I look up at Doña Marcela, a blurry figure high in those mountains. She puts a hand to her heart.

Dolor, she whispers. I can hear her as if she were standing right next to me, whispering in my ear.

Dolor, she says again.

And I close my eyes, letting the fresh pain wash over me, saturating every part of me. I feel my mother's kiss on my face, her hand on my cheek, gentle in a way it never was in real life.

And I cry.

And I mourn

all the things that could've been,

and all the things that were.

• • •

Paulo is in the kitchen with his grandmother. I hear them talking in low voices and then Paulo is looking over at me.

"Hey," he says as he comes and sits at the end of the couch. I pull my feet up so there's room. "You okay? How'd you sleep?"

I look at him. *I fought a bear except he didn't fight back. Your grandmother was there. I think she's the one who gathered us all. . . .*

I try to make sense of everything.

"I should go," I tell Paulo. "I have to see Shelly." I worry she's still out in the desert, crying. I wonder if the bear came back for her. I don't remember how my dream ended.

Paulo moves closer. "Don't worry about Shelly," he says. "I drove over there this morning, told her you were here. She came by to check on you but didn't want to wake you up."

"I gotta go," I insist.

"I'll give you a ride."

"I'll walk."

He looks at me doubtfully.

"I'll go straight to her house," I tell him. "The sun's not hot and . . . I just have to walk." I offer him a small smile.

He nods. "All right."

I get up and head outside. He grabs my hand, and when he pulls me close to him, my eyes fill with tears.

"What's wrong?"

"Nothing," I tell him.

"Come on, let me walk you home, at least," he says. I stare at the road leading to Shelly's. The same dusty road my mom walked so many times.

I shake my head. "I'm fine, really."

"Okay, but you're going straight to Shelly's, right?"

"I promise."

He watches me go.

And as I set my feet on that road and walk, I look for the bear around every bend. I wait for him to emerge from a bush and charge me.

"Hey, Dani!" I hear. "Dani!" It takes me a few seconds to process the voices, to see the dark silhouettes that keep calling to me.

It's Jessie and Chicken. They wave and tell me to

hurry up or I'm gonna miss the bus. I shake my head and they keep calling but I ignore them.

My brain is like a dial on a radio and it tunes in to a Patsy Cline song, and I look over to the mountains and wait for the ground to tremble.

But nothing.

Just Patsy's voice.

And my mom. She's who I feel. Some version of her that once existed. Some version of her that never existed. Walking with me.

• • •

Shelly is sitting at the kitchen table when I get home. She watches me come in and I sit down across from her.

"You . . . okay?" she asks.

I nod. "I'm sorry . . . if I worried you," I tell her.

She sighs and looks at the wall on the far side of the kitchen. "When I got home, I thought you'd gone back to the trailer. I looked for you there first, but then . . ." She shakes her head. "I thought maybe you'd left. . . ."

It takes me a minute to understand she means left like my mom left.

"I couldn't sleep . . . ," I explain.

"Paulo came just when I was getting in the truck." She sighs again. "I don't even know where I was headed, but I knew I was going after you, the way I would've gone after your mom if I'd known. . . ." Her red eyes fill with fresh tears, making my own eyes hurt. She lets out a breath. "God, Dani, you look so much like her," she says, staring at me.

I can see how much Shelly misses her. I want to ask if she dreamed what I did, but I don't know how.

We sit in silence. "She loved you, you know . . . ," Shelly says suddenly.

I think of all the times Mom looked at me with anger, with that look that seemed to ask why she ever had me. Shelly couldn't know if Mom really loved me or not. "She hated me . . . ," I tell her.

"We were full of hate, Dani. I know she was. I have been too. Hate and anger and . . . loneliness. All that bad blood, it runs in our veins." Shelly lets out another sigh, one that seems to echo off the bare walls and through the empty hallways. The house feels even emptier somehow.

I look at Shelly, the way she stares off into nothingness, the way she has surrounded herself with nothingness. And I think of how she hasn't let anyone into her life; she never brought anyone into this world. I think of how Shelly has cut herself off from everyone. Everything.

I suddenly remember reading somewhere about a man who was infected with rabies and tied himself to a tree so he wouldn't hurt anyone else. An image of Shelly tied to a tree, foaming at the mouth, whips into my mind. And another, of her out here in the desert by herself, bleeding that bad blood into the desert floor, fills my head. It scares me to think of her that way. It makes it hard to breathe. I push the images out of my mind and focus on her face. Despite the stern lines on her face, there's a softness in her eyes as she speaks.

No, Shelly isn't bleeding to death. She isn't tied to trees. She has withstood the unthinkable. She reminds me of Paulo's grandmother. I want to tell her that, but suddenly I see something so clearly.

She let me in.

My chest tightens and I suck in my breath at the realization.

"Are you okay?" She reaches across the table and takes my hand in hers.

She closed out the whole world. But she let me in. I nod. "Fine," I say. She gives me a worried smile.

"I'm not making excuses for her," Shelly continues. "I just know she loved you. I know she probably wanted to do right by you. She just didn't know how. I feel . . . like she's asking me to do right by you now."

Her eyes fill with even more tears. "It's difficult to understand how you can hate somebody, wish they were dead even, and yet still cling to them and feel them with you. It doesn't make sense. It feels wrong to love them and it feels wrong to hate them." She looks like she's trying to figure it out herself. "You might spend the rest of your life trying to make sense of it."

You might hide yourself away, tie yourself to a tree, dwell in an empty house.

My eyes fill with tears.

Shelly takes a deep breath. "It's not fair that she wasn't a good mom. But there *was* goodness in your mother once, when I knew her. Before all that other crap piled up over it. There was goodness there. And that part loved you." She looks like she doesn't want to go on, but she forces herself to ask, "Did you . . . did you ever see that side of her?"

She looks at me and I try to answer. I try to remember. Maybe my mother tried, but it always turned bad and she blamed me for it. She always said it was me who ruined everything. And I believed her.

Shelly searches my eyes and I turn away because now I keep seeing it, that kindness, that softness. For me.

I remember instead how Mom's eyes looked when she drank. Like she was glad not to feel anything at all, to be numb and dull. But there was more underneath that. Hate. Disgust. Disappointment.

But maybe it wasn't for me.

Maybe it was for herself.

I look at the emptiness around me.

Maybe Mom just wanted room to breathe, like Shelly.

Isn't this better?

But maybe for Mom the past was too loud in all that space. Maybe it screamed and clattered and told her who she was, who she would always be, what she couldn't escape.

Maybe only the liquor muffled the past.

Maybe it hid the part that wanted to do right by me.

Maybe all of it was just too much for the good part to fight through.

"Did you ever see that part of her? The good part?" Shelly asks again.

I look at Shelly. "I . . . I don't know," I tell her. I feel panicked and scared. Because looking at Shelly and trying to remember makes my heart quiver with too much emotion. It makes me feel love and hate and too many things I can't define.

I shake my head. "I don't know," I repeat. Shelly nods and tells me it's okay. And we sit there. With too much. In all that emptiness.

• • •

Days and weeks pass. I go to school. I make more slashes on the calendar, watch September start filling up. But time keeps passing without me. Even as I try to pin it down, it keeps going while I feel stuck.

I feel like the bear failed me. All this time he was pushing me, urging me to find out about the past. As if it would bring some kind of enlightenment. But all I learned is how screwed up my mom's life was and how that made her a screwed-up person and a screwed-up mom. And then the bear just disappeared. I don't know if I'm glad or if I miss rounding each corner to find him there. All I know is that knowing all those things about Mom doesn't make anything easier. It makes it harder.

And I hate her more because she never told me.

And I hate her less because I think of her in that trailer all those years ago.

But she's not reachable. She never was and never will be. Because it's too late.

I tell Paulo. I tell him everything. I tell him I was a superhero in my dream, that I defeated the bear. I pretend I drop-kicked the bear and levitated and beat him, like Keanu Reeves in *The Matrix*. And shouldn't that count for something? Shouldn't life be easier now? Except I didn't do any of that. The bear lay down and died and left me with more questions than answers.

Paulo tells me you never really bury your past, that it always comes back and haunts you. And there are never any ends, just the beginnings of something else. So I keep searching for the something else.

I haven't picked up *The Stranger* in a while, but sometimes I remember Meursault. A part of me hates him and his unfeeling ways, because it's a lie. The world won't let you go through life unscathed. It insists you feel every burn. It insists you pay attention. Even if you're stumbling the whole way. Falling. Almost dead.

There's a pep rally at school. The music thumps into the bleachers and the players come running into the gymnasium. And then the bear comes running, wearing a T-shirt and dancing. He waves and break-dances and everyone goes wild. He jumps and spins around and around. He lashes out at us with his paws. He nods like he knows something we don't.

You forgot to tell me something! I yell at him. *You forgot to tell me what to do!* But he doesn't listen. He can't hear me over all the other screaming. He doesn't even look at me.

But I watch him. I keep my eyes on him the whole time and when he goes to the locker room afterward, I wait outside the door. It's the end of the day. Everyone is dismissed. *Go home. Go home.*

The players emerge, laughing and joking and giving each other high fives. And when I'm sure they're gone, I go in.

I look around, wondering where the bear can be.

Now it's me, I tell him, *me coming for you.* I walk past locker after locker. I peek inside the coach's office. Nothing.

Where are you hiding?

I walk past showers and wooden benches, bags with basketballs, and stacked orange cones. And then I see a large storage closet at the end of the room.

I walk to it, stand there a moment before opening the door.

There he is, his mouth open in a silent growl. His teeth white and sharp. His tongue velvety red. A bodiless bear's head.

This time, I'm here for you, I tell him, and he stares back at me with that frozen menacing look.

I reach out, touch the black cotton fur of his face. He doesn't flinch. I stick my hand in his mouth. He doesn't bite. I lift his head and bring it closer to me, look at his plastic eyes and leather nose. Nothing. He is empty and lifeless and I don't know what else I expected.

I look around and when I get the urge to put it on, I do. I lower it over my head, the smell of sweat filling my nose and an uncomfortable warmth caressing my face.

I can hear myself breathing, heavy, like I've been running.

I take the head off. I want to steal it. I don't know why, but I do. I want to take it home and keep it in the corner of my closet where I can keep an eye on it. So I'll know when the bear comes alive again.

I go to the office. I tell them I missed my bus and need to call for a ride. And I call Paulo, who closes the gas station and says he'll be there soon. And when I see his truck pulling into the school parking lot, I run to the locker room, grab the head, and sprint like hell to the truck.

I only sort of register Paulo's words and the way he looks at me when I get in. I only sort of wonder what he must think as I tell him *Drive!*

• • •

I put the bear head on the kitchen table, stare at it until it doesn't make sense, and then leave it there. I go to my room and lie down.

It gets darker and I keep telling myself to *Get up, get up and hide it!*

But then Shelly comes home. I hear her footsteps as she enters the house, the way they stop when she must have laid eyes on the head. And then I wait for her to come and find me. It feels like forever.

"Why is that bear head on the table?" she says in the darkness of the hallway.

My eyes fill with tears. I want to tell her the reasons, because there were reasons. I know I took it for a reason, but I can't make sense of it. I don't know how to tell her because I can't remember why anymore.

"I had to" is all I say. It isn't a good reason, but it is the truth.

She leans against the doorframe and stays quiet for a long time.

I don't think Shelly knows what the hell to do now. I don't think she knew what to do when they were young, and she didn't know what to do when her family exploded, when they shot out in all different directions and only she survived. And I don't think she knows what to do with me, a piece of Anna Ruby projected back.

"Dani . . . ," she says.

"I . . . I'm trying," I tell her. "I'm trying to make sense of everything."

"I know," Shelly says. "I know you are. I'm sorry. . . ."

I wipe my eyes. "It's not your fault."

Shelly starts crying then, softly and with her head down, but I hear her. And it makes more tears slide out of my own eyes. She comes in, sits at the foot of my bed. She bends over in a way that reminds me of the Atlas lotería card, the whole world on her shoulders, and I worry that whatever peace Shelly has made with the past, I've gone and dug it all up. Now she has to figure out what to do with the dead body all over again.

I sit up, put one hand on her shoulder.

"*I'm* sorry . . . ," I tell her as she keeps crying. "I'm sorry I'm here. I've brought it all back."

Only the light from the hallway offers any light in my room, but I catch the expression on Shelly's face when she grabs my hand and turns to look at me.

"Don't you ever think that," she says through clenched teeth. I'm scared she's angry, but she caresses my hand and holds it to her face. "I'm so glad you're here. So glad you exist. So glad Anna carried you . . ." She tries to get through the words. "So glad that I have this chance to do right by her."

Her tears wet my hand, and something in me, some hard rock that has been lodged in my heart forever shifts a little.

. . .

A few days after I leave the bear head on the table, Shelly says we have to talk to a therapist.

I'm worried Shelly might go to jail for helping her mother bury her father's body all those years ago. For never telling anyone. We look up laws on the Internet anxiously and hold on to hope. We think she won't be charged because she was a minor. So we go.

Over the next month, she starts telling Dr. Marques everything.

I do too.

It goes something like this:

"I'm trying to forgive her."

"Maybe you're not ready to forgive your mother yet."

Silence.

"Not forgiving her makes me feel bad. How can you not forgive a dead person, but also, how can you? They're fucking dead." I'm angry, the way I used to be when my mom was around. I remember how I hated carrying all that anger with me. It's exhausting.

"Are you upset?"

I laugh. "Yes."

"Can you tell me why?"

Silence. Then, "Because she died." Dr. Marques looks at me. She wants more. There's more of an answer here and it's coming together in my mind, in my chest, and becoming words. "And because I never got to tell her how fucked up she was, and now she's gone and I'm the one who has to deal with it."

Heat creeps into my face and I look at Dr. Marques. She nods in that way that means *keep going.*

"I didn't get to say that, but I wanted to so many times and now I can't. And I'm pissed that I *want* to tell her she was fucked up. I know it's because she went through so much. But she never explained anything. Never. So it made *me* feel fucked up. And that's how it always was. She was fucked up, she did fucked-up things, but *I, I* was the one who felt fucked up. It's not fair."

Dr. Lopez nods again. "It's not," she says. "But it's certainly not too late for you."

And I start to cry. Because I cry all the time now.

And I think of how my whole life, I fought against being like my mother, surrounding herself with false love. And I think of Shelly, dwelling in that big house all alone, not letting anyone in.

What would happen to me?

"I don't want to hate her. I don't want to be full of hate," I say through my tears. "I want to forgive her. But . . ."

"What makes it so hard to forgive her, Dani?"

Silence.

"She never asked," I say finally. "Her father did wrong by her, but my mom . . . she did wrong by me."

Silence.

"And she never asked for my forgiveness. She

didn't even think to ask. And now she's off the hook. But I have to forgive her even though I hated her. Because . . ."

Silence.

"Because what, Dani? Why do you want to forgive her? Try to put the feelings into words."

"Because . . ." *Because forgiving her will make me feel better. Because somehow it means we were really mother and daughter. She really gave birth to me. Once, she really carried me in her arms. Once, she really . . . loved me.*

"Because . . . I loved her."

"Okay."

"I loved her."

Dr. Marques nods.

"And because I just . . . wanted to be enough."

"Enough for what?"

"I don't know. . . ." Silence. *Enough so that it wouldn't matter that I made her into something maybe she didn't want to be. A mother. Enough so that she changed her mind. Enough so that all that happened before I was born was worth me, was worth me being born.*

"Enough for what?"

Silence.

Enough so she wouldn't hate me.

"Just enough. I wanted to be enough."

Dr. Marques nods again and the session is over.

• • •

Paulo is in my room. The bear head is in the corner.

"You gonna keep that?" he asks.

I look at it. I took it out of the closet last week. I don't know why I want it somewhere where I can see it as soon as I walk into the room. It makes Shelly uneasy; I can see the way her eyes brush over it when she comes in my room for some reason or other. But she doesn't tell me to get rid of it.

"I guess," I tell Paulo. He sits down on my bed and looks at it.

"Has he come back?" he says.

I shake my head.

"Are you worried he will?"

I remember the way the bear fell into that great hole. The way I've tried to conjure him up and he doesn't come.

"No."

I sit down next to Paulo and stare at the fuzzy head. The open mouth.

"How'd you get through it?" I ask him.

"What?"

"Your parents."

Paulo takes a deep breath. "I'm not through it," he says. "It's part of me. Sometimes it still feels huge and fresh, and sometimes it feels like it happened to someone else. But . . ." He smiles.

It makes me smile, the way Paulo smiles.

"What?"

"It's stupid."

"Tell me."

He looks at me, his eyes filled with sadness.

"I figure I can't change it. And it can make me good or bad, but I want to be good. I want to have good in my life. I want to be el valiente."

"El valiente . . ."

He laughs, poses like he has a sword in his hand, and looks to one side like some kind of warrior.

I laugh, and he looks at me and suddenly says, "Dani, you're beautiful."

I look away, because no one has ever told me I'm beautiful. And the way he says it, the way he looks at me, makes me believe him, this guy I have feelings for and who actually seems to care for me. I shake my head.

"You are . . . ," he says. And he brings his face close to mine and presses his lips against my lips. The way we kiss, it's as if we are breathing together, and I think, *I want to have good in my life too.* Maybe I can be el valiente too.

I can face the world and all it gives me.

I can carry it on my shoulders and still stand.

I can remember her without hating her.

I can know that somewhere, sometime, I was—am—loved.

Paulo pulls away. "I remember the first day I saw you," he says.

My mind flashes with images of the sun, the store, Paulo, and pink.

I look down, remembering.

"Hey," he says suddenly. "I want to do something." I think he means go somewhere, but he gets up and grabs the bear head.

"Can I borrow this?"

"What?"

"I'll give it back. I just . . . I want to do something. And it's just for you."

I look at the bear head, the way it's tucked under Paulo's arm. I don't think I want it out of my sight.

"It'll just be for a day . . . two days. And I'll bring it back. Please."

"Okay. . . ."

"Great." He kisses me again. "I'll give it back in two days . . . maybe three. . . ."

"Three?"

"I promise . . . I just . . . You'll see." He makes his way to the door.

"Now?" I want him to stay.

"Yeah, I'll . . . it's a surprise."

And he's out the door and gone.

• • •

Three days later, the bear head is back. In the corner of my room. Like it never left. Paulo dropped it off at night, didn't even come in, just handed it to me and told me we'd meet up after school the next day.

"Okay, now will you tell me what's going on?" I

ask him when I get off the school bus and he is there, waiting for me.

"Not yet."

Jessie and Chicken look at us and smile like they're in on the secret.

They watch, walking backward and blocking their eyes from the sun, as Paulo and I drive off in the opposite direction, the dust an orange screen between us.

"Where are we going?" I ask.

Paulo doesn't look at me, just keeps driving, his eyes on the road. "You'll see."

We head toward Deming, away from the border. We don't stop until we get to some buildings on the side of the road, buildings I've never bothered to find out about. They just stand there, in the middle of nowhere, abandoned.

"Here?" I ask Paulo.

He slows down, stops, puts the truck in park, and shuts off the engine.

"Yep," he says. He gets out of the truck and goes around to the back, gets a box I didn't notice before, and gestures for me to follow him.

As we walk, he tells me about the place. "This was an old movie set. They shot *Sonny Boy* here, this crazy movie with David Carradine, back in the late eighties. You ever seen it?"

I shake my head. "But I know who David Carradine is."

He smiles. "Cool. Anyway, the movie studio built

the set hoping to film more movies here. But that's the only one that was."

"Is it any good?"

Paulo gets this look on his face like his head is going to explode.

"It's one of the most fantastically bizarre movies I've ever seen. But yeah, it's good. The fact that a lot of people disagree makes me love it even more. It's just crazy, with this kid who gets his tongue cut out and . . ." He explains the movie. I love the way he looks as he tells me everything about it. How his face and his whole body grow more animated, like movies are blood, the essence of life.

I want to tell him I love him, and then I feel stupid, so I say, "So what, now the set is just here?"

Paulo nods. "Yep, crew packed up and left and we got this."

I look around. "Are we allowed to be here?"

"Of course. Why wouldn't we be?"

He heads toward a patio with a large, cream-colored stucco wall.

"Right here," he says, putting the box down. I watch as he pulls a blanket out of the box, then a computer, wires, and extension cords, and what looks like a projector.

"What are you doing?" I ask.

"I'll be right back," he says, and before I can ask anything else, he takes off running.

I look around. At the crumbling walls, the way this

particular spot is basically a three-walled room with a half ceiling and a cement floor. There is a cutout for a door, but no door. From the outside, the set looks like an old Southwestern structure, but this side is completely unfinished, empty and bare but shaded.

I see Paulo making his way back, dragging a generator. He sets it up far away from me and plugs the projector and computer into it.

I watch as he turns the empty box around, sets the projector on top of it, and then looks at me nervously.

"What the hell are you doing?" I ask, laughing at the elaborate setup. "Is it the Carradine flick? We could've watched it at my house."

He laughs and shakes his head. "Nah, nothing like that. I mean . . . I wanted to show you it here"—he gestures at the desert—"in the middle of nowhere. In the most desolate of places. Because . . . there's something beautiful about you seeing it out here."

He's fidgety and I wait to see if he says more. Finally, he reaches over and grabs my hand. In that moment I think of how when Paulo grew a new heart, he grew a beautiful one.

He looks at me and says, "I'm really glad I met you. I'm glad you're here."

I'm embarrassed and touched and I can feel myself getting hot the way I do when I don't know what to do.

"I'm glad I met you, too," I tell him, and I think what these months would've been like without him. I never looked to him for saving. I was never going to be my mother. He didn't save me. But he was there when I needed someone.

He looks at me and says, "This is for you."

And he starts the movie.

• • •

The first time I see her, I'm watching Pulp Fiction *and I've got the newspaper spread out on the counter. I'm reading the terrible news about the border and the drugs and the guns. . . .*

Paulo is narrating and there's a shot of him at the gas station, just like I saw him that day. He's even wearing the same clothes. There's a newspaper in front of him and then close-ups of the newspaper, the date . . . quick cuts to the violent headlines about murders and found corpses and the newspaper stack piling up, up, up. Then back to Paulo, standing at the counter.

I try not to be apathetic about that shit, because apathy is dangerous and it's easy to be that way when violence is constant. I look up because if you look out at the land, at the orange earth and blue sky, you can leave some room in your brain to think about the world being beautiful instead of so fucked.

The screen fills with fast-forward shots of orange earth and blue skies, flowers growing, and the sun rising and setting.

So I'm reading the paper when I look up to glance

outside and that's when I see her. Walking toward the gas station, all stumbling and shaky.

I watch as Jessie comes on-screen, wearing jean shorts and a yellow T-shirt, just like I was wearing that day ... I didn't even remember until just now. I feel my heart beating faster, anticipating and not knowing what will appear on the screen next.

I saw this movie once, I forget which one it was, where this guy suddenly sees the girl of his dreams. Shit, that's because it's every movie, right?

Clips of movies with couples meeting romantically follow, as Paulo continues to narrate.

The whole slow-motion bit, as the guy is dumbstruck and the camera zooms in on the girl laughing with someone or at something, pushing her hair behind her ears all shy-like, and then it zooms in on the idiot guy just standing there and staring until the girl suddenly looks right at him. Only at him.

That's how it happens in shit movies, and that's why they're shit. That's not the way things go down when you're out in the middle of nowhere.

Back to a shot of Paulo at the gas station counter.

No, no, this went down so different. She walks in looking like she's come straight out of hell. Like a fucked-up heavy-metal song.

More fast-forward shots that feel chaotic and out of sync as the camera tries to zoom in on Jessie, on me.

She's red and sweaty and her eyes are dull and her hair flies around her like birds have been pulling at the strands.

And she walks up and down the aisles, staring at everything on the shelves. But she's empty. An emptiness that comes through in her eyes.

Shot of Paulo watching me.

And then she steals gum.

I watch as Jessie pockets the gum just like I did, the little plastic squares tucked between her fingers and then slid into her pocket. I watch as she walks down some more aisles and then out the door, as she peels a piece of gum open and puts it in her mouth.

And then she goes in the desert and fucking passes out.

Shit . . . now, that's how it happens in a Robert Rodriguez or Quentin Tarantino movie. That's how it happened to me. That's how I fall for her.

Shot of Paulo's face, close-up, and then he grabs a water bottle and runs out of the gas station.

And then a shot of me, coming in and drinking soda.

Another shot of me, taking the calendar and more gum.

I don't say anything to her because that's the way my guy in a movie would play it. I just watch her steal and then I watch her go. Because I know I'll see her again.

Another shot of me, looking over at him.

Another shot of me, standing in the desert.

A shot of the sun going down as I stand staring at it.

Then the sun rising on me.

And then a shot of a pair of feet in dusty sneakers walking.

And walking.

The sound of gravel and dust.

And more walking, fast and slow, fast and slow.

Until finally the sneakers stop.

I knew when I met her, I knew I'd make a movie about it all.

The camera pans over, and suddenly the bear head comes into view.

But the bear has flowers where its eyes should be. Flowers in every color coming out of its mouth. Petals and sugar skulls surround it.

All that was ferocious about it has disappeared. Now it's this thing of strange beauty.

But this is as far as I can take it. This is what I've witnessed. The rest, only she knows.

The camera pans back to the dusty sneakers and then zooms out until both the bear head and sneakers are in the shot. And then it fades to black.

I sit there, looking at the stucco wall. I feel how my body has tensed, how my fists are clenched so hard my hands hurt. And I tell myself to breathe because I don't think I will otherwise.

We sit in silence. We sit with only the sound of the generator in the background.

We sit and we breathe.

I finally look over at Paulo and I see how hard it is for him not to say anything. I can see how he wants to ask me if I liked it, if I know why he shot some of the angles the way he did, if I noticed the lotería cards he placed in some of the scenes that only I would ever understand. I know he wants to ask me everything, but I can't speak. I can't say anything at all.

So I kiss him. And I kiss him. And I kiss him.

• • •

The next morning, Shelly is at the kitchen table when I walk in.

"Long night?" I ask her. If she's up it's because she never went to bed after returning from her night shift.

She nods but says nothing, just looks at me like she did when I first got here.

"What's wrong?" I ask, tensing up.

She shakes her head. "Nothing. I was just thinking . . . I've been here my whole life. Never even been on a plane."

I wait. It's not like her to be indirect or stretch out whatever is on her mind.

"I was thinking . . . you have a couple of days off from school coming up. We could go to Florida."

I take a deep breath. Florida. My mind instantly fills with the ocean. But I don't want to be there. For now I want to stay where it is bare, where there is nothing to hide from. Where there is hierbabuena. Where bears have been buried and sprouted flowers.

I start shaking. I can feel my arms and legs being pumped with adrenaline that is supposed to make me stronger but somehow makes me feel weak and shaky.

"Florida . . . ," I whisper.

Shelly nods.

I'm worried we will become nomads. I'm worried this is the beginning of a bunch of apartments that will be too small, of houses that will be too big. Of pools and large backyards that meet with forests and hide bears.

But Shelly says we'll go for a week and come back.

So we go.

• • •

On the plane, I finish reading *The Stranger*. I grabbed it from the drawer because I knew Meursault had to make the trip back to Florida with me, even if I'd abandoned him. He was tucked away in my backpack again, but he kept calling me, telling me to get him off the beach. To get the gun out of his hand. So I do.

And now I know Meursault's fate. The one that had seemed inescapable when I stopped reading and put the book away.

I wanted him to somehow get his freedom, like Andy. I wanted him to escape. I needed him to. But something warned me he wouldn't and now I knew. He was going to jail to wait out the days before being executed. And worse, he'd lose his head.

I close the book and try not to think of Meursault on the chopping block.

I wish Meursault's fate were different. I see him lying on his prison cot, surrounded by gray cement blocks, staring at the ceiling, and I almost cry because maybe it could have been different. He tells me it doesn't matter, that none of it means anything.

I let him believe that, even though I don't.

I tell this fictional character who seems so real that it's okay to cry. I turn his head to the sun.

I slip Andy's rock hammer and a rolled-up Rita Hayworth poster under his pillow, just in case.

And I leave.

I look over at Shelly.

My grandmother is with us. In a blue and green urn. Shelly, normally steady and no-nonsense, is a fucking mess, like she's had too many Red Bulls or something. More than once, I grab her hand and hold it, which seems to calm her down.

She makes me think of the lady on the plane with bad breath and I crack a smile, but Shelly doesn't notice.

She's looking out the window and I feel like I should tell her, all we have is each other. I feel like I should tell her that when I look at her hands and see the blue veins in them, I think of her blood and my blood and how we share the same blood and how Mom did too, and her mama did also, and even my grandfather, who was terrible but now I can't help but wonder what made him so terrible, and how we all come from the same place. The same place. But we all go out in different directions.

She turns and looks at me and I smile.

"You okay?" she asks, even though she's the one who doesn't look okay.

I nod.

And I hold her hand. And I see how she clutches the bag that holds Grandma.

Grandma.

I shake my head. And I start laughing even though I know it's wrong, because I'm thinking, *I'm on an airplane with Grandma*, and it's such a little-kid thought.

But I'm not a little kid.

And my grandma is in an urn.

The pilot tells us to prepare for landing.

• • •

Even in October, Florida is the same. Hot, sticky, and humid. We get in the rental car and blast the air-conditioning and drive to our hotel.

We settle in our room. And then we eat dinner. And we talk about what we'll do.

We won't go to theme parks.

We won't see ridiculous characters.

We will visit my mother.

We will "tie things up," is the way Shelly puts it.

But I know what it really is. It's our last grand

gesture of love. It's us walking like Pérez until we pass out, until we fall. So we can get up again and go on.

I keep catching glimpses of Shelly out of the corner of my eye, walking next to me. I keep thinking it's strange, the way we are navigating through the world. Months ago, she was a stranger, and now she's the person by my side. She's the person with me at my mother's grave. She's the person talking to my mom, telling her things I thought only I felt.

Like how she would've done anything for her.

Like how much she hates her and everything she put her through.

But how much she loves her.

And how much she misses her.

And how she wanted so bad to understand her.

But didn't.

How she failed her.

And how she failed us, too.

I let Shelly speak because she has the words and because when I saw the small postcard someone had thought to wrap in cellophane and tuck against the headstone, I started crying too much and too hard to say anything other than *I love you*. And when I pulled from my pocket the miniature cross I'd bought in Mexico and placed it next to the postcard, I cried even harder. Because she *had* mattered. Her life *had* meant something. And her death hurt me more deeply than anything in my whole life.

Because she had been my mother.

Shelly takes out a large plastic bag full of sand and rocks.

I wipe my nose, take a deep breath. "What's that?"

Shelly doesn't look up. "Grandma," she says.

I look at the little shell-like fragments of bone and dust that made up my grandmother. I hear the rolling pebbles from New Mexico under my feet.

"I found her, Mama. Here is Anna Ruby Falls," Shelly says to Grandma as she pours her remains on top of Mom's grave. She shakes her head. "No, actually, Anna Ruby came back to us." She looks at me and I look at her and I think of all Shelly has lost as she reaches for my hand.

"We'll get a new headstone," she says. "We'll get Anna Ruby Falls engraved on it."

I nod, wondering when Mom must have legally changed her name. When had she decided she was Ruby? When had she stopped being Anna?

We stand there for a long while, until the sun shines through the tree branches and Meursault's last words to the judge echo in my ears.

It was because of the sun, he answers when the judge asks him why he killed the man. That's all he says, the only explanation he offers before he is sentenced to death. It's a ridiculous answer. Nobody understands and they laugh at him. But his words aren't ridiculous to me; they swirl in my head and my heart.

It *was* because of the sun.

Because it was hot and melted your brain. Because

it was an absurd ball of fire in the sky that blinded us and regulated our days and nights, our seemingly senseless lives and random fates.

Because smaller suns found their way into the wombs of women. Who knows why or how they chose which wombs, which mother, which father to whom they were ultimately delivered.

Yes, it was because of the sun. The ones that found their way into her womb and released me into the world.

It makes sense to me; Meursault makes sense to me. I think of him in his jail cell, waiting for death, refusing God and religion and the world, convincing himself everything is for nothing, and even that makes sense to me. Because his heart is dead. Because he refuses to grow another one.

But I have to believe there's more. More than just burning. More than just blind apathy. I have to believe that sometimes there is relief and a little bit of goodness.

I look at Mom's grave and the sea of headstones around us and the trees standing tall, their branches full and slightly swaying, and I realize *Sometimes there is shade, there is respite, there is beauty and love.*

Remember to seek shade, I tell myself. And we stand there and I tell myself over and over, *Remember to seek shade.*

Shelly takes a deep breath and looks at me. I stare back at her and think if Mom had never died, I would never have known Shelly. And I feel bad because I'm glad I do; I'm glad I know Aunt Shelly. That's how I think of her now, as my aunt, my blood. My mother's sister. I'm glad I'm with her and she's next to me. So what does that mean? I shake my head and start crying again. *Because I loved you, too.*

I close my eyes and I think I feel my mother telling me it's okay. And I wonder if making sure Aunt Shelly and I found each other, even though she never told us that the other existed, was somehow Mom's last grand gesture of love. A love she never knew how to show when she was alive.

I don't know if it's wishful thinking, but I decide it'll be what I believe.

"What now?" I ask.

"Now?" Aunt Shelly says. "I guess let's get the hell out of here."

And we do, we get the hell out of there. But before we go, I take a good look at Mom's grave because I don't know when I'll be back.

Ruby Falls. That's who she was to me. She kept Anna hidden. But Anna was always there.

• • •

We spend the rest of the week "tying things up." We visit Helen. We look at the outside of the house where Mom and I lived. Where she died. And we take the boxes that Helen packed up and stored at her house, filled with my and Mom's whole life, and drive back to New Mexico in a U-Haul.

Aunt Shelly seems tough as she navigates the truck. The nervousness I detected in her at the airport is gone, and she's back to the way she usually is.

"Is it weird, Aunt Shelly?" I ask her as we head onto the highway.

"What's that?" she asks, and I don't know if she hears me call her *Aunt* or if she's responding to the question I've asked.

"Knowing where she lived, where she existed without you?"

Aunt Shelly is quiet for a while. "It is weird. It makes me miss her."

"What was it like afterward," I press on, "when it was just you and Grandma?"

We hit a pothole and the truck shakes violently. We bounce up from the seat and crash down again. Aunt Shelly's hands grip the wheel tighter and she takes her time before she answers.

"It was like the silence after something very loud. An eerie kind of quiet that fills your ears. And stillness. Everything was so still that we both got in the habit of doing everything carefully, more carefully than before, whether it was turning the faucet on so the water barely trickled out, or closing and opening a door with only the faintest click." She shakes her head. "Our secret, their absence, was so thick in the air, Mama couldn't breathe. She just ran out of air."

I look at her. "What about you?"

"I don't know. . . ." She keeps her eyes on the road. "The same, I guess," she whispers, and she keeps driving.

I nod and then we turn on the radio.

On the second night, when the roads aren't too full and it's dark except for the bright light of the headlights on the road in front of us, Aunt Shelly asks me how bad it was.

When I tell her, it somehow seems really bad and not so bad. I wonder if that's how survival works. Like a bad dream that seems so real. Or something so piercing and real, it has to get hazy and blurry around the edges before you can stand to remember it.

"She just wasn't happy," I say. "I couldn't make her happy. And then I stopped trying."

"That wasn't your job," Aunt Shelly says. And I think about that until we reach a gas station, where we fuel up and get back on the road.

• • •

We drive into New Mexico as the sun is coming up. And I'm surprised by the comfort the brown landscape brings. I'm reminded of the first time Aunt Shelly and I drove through here together, when she picked me up from the airport.

I look over at her. She's familiar. She's family. She's

my aunt and my mom and our whole past, where there's too much bad but also some goodness.

"Aunt Shelly," I say.

"Hmm?"

"I love you." I say it fast, before I can stop myself or change my mind or my mouth can stumble over the strange, unpracticed words.

She looks at me. "I love you too, Dani. I've loved you since you were born."

"You didn't know I existed."

"Doesn't matter," she says.

And somehow I know what she means. "I'm glad I have you. I'm glad I found you, Aunt Shelly." She smiles and her face and eyes are so bright.

We drive into Columbus, past the abandoned film set where Paulo showed the movie he made for me, past border control agents who check the cars coming in the opposite direction, past Paulo and Doña Marcela's trailer, toward the barn that houses our past, toward a house that holds our future.

We get out and I hear the pebbles rolling under our feet as we walk toward the door.

Aunt Shelly opens the door and we go inside. It's still as bare as the first day I got here, but it feels like coming home. And I see it like a movie. I see us filling it up in the next few days as we unpack the boxes in the truck and in the barn that reveal what we've been through, of those who have come before us, who don't scare us, who don't haunt us. Of the things we have kept hidden and are no longer afraid of.

I don't want to believe it was all for nothing.

It was for something. It meant something, all of it. Because it was us. Because we survived.

I feel a shuddering in my chest and wonder if it is my old heart reviving or a new one being born. I look at Aunt Shelly dragging in a suitcase, and when she looks at me, she smiles, and I think about her heart. Our hearts. The possibility of them growing. Infinitely.

"We survived," she says to me, and I know she must mean more than the long trip home.

Because we survived the burning sun,
and the past,
and vicious bears,
and even ourselves.

"We did more than survive, Aunt Shelly," I tell her.

Now we're like the flowers sprouting from the bear's mouth.

I read *The Stranger* for the first time as a senior in high school. It was a class assignment. Maybe that was just the right time for it to stick, because it is a book I have never been able to shake. I was pretty jaded at seventeen. The world seemed confusing and hopeless and absurd. When I met Camus's Meursault, he was the kind of fascinating character I couldn't ignore.

I wanted to figure him out. I wanted to make sense of and understand his detachment from the world. I especially wondered about his relationship with his mother. We never learn much about her or how she and Meursault interacted in life, but his reaction to her death immediately made me wonder, what could make him so detached from his mother, from her death, that he can't grieve for her? Some part of me thought maybe she was a terrible mother to him, though there's no evidence she was.

Over the years I've read and reread the novel. I've daydreamed and imagined Meursault as a child living with this terrible woman. I believed I knew how she must have made him feel, even while I understood that most likely she was never meant to be anything other than a typical mother. No better or worse than most. The idea of a complicated and fractured parent-child relationship never left me, however.

One day I found myself writing about a girl who was disturbingly detached from the reality of her mother being mauled to death by a bear. Suddenly there was Meursault. He was lingering in the shadows of my story, hands in pockets. I imagined him looking over at Dani as if he understood her. And when she picks up the book she's supposed to read over the summer for school, it's *The Stranger*. Immediately, I thought, Okay, you two, let's see what will happen here. Let's see how you are similar. And perhaps more importantly, how you are different.

Because Dani and Meursault *had* to be different. I knew that.

I've carried Meursault with me for years, in various backpacks and tote bags. I've kept several copies of *The Stranger* on my bookshelves because sometimes I can't resist buying it again with a new cover.

Meursault speaks to the part of me that is at odds with the world. He's the one who says, "Come on," and shows me the world through dark-tinted glasses. Somehow that view helps me make sense of it. He points to numbness and despair, injustice and apathy. He shows me rejection. These things are valid; they exist.

But when I was writing *Because of the Sun*, I realized that the problem with Meursault is that he *never* takes off those glasses. So even his enlightenment is dark. Or is it enlightenment at all?

It was important that Dani's story be honest, and not only that she recognize the tragedy that was weaving itself into her life long before she was born, but that she see and experience goodness. For me, goodness, beauty, and hope can exist even in the darkest places, and I wanted readers to know this. So Dani becomes someone who ultimately sees the world in its juxtaposed glory: pain and relief, hate and love, cruelty and kindness. And the perfect setting for her to come to this understanding was a place I feel embodies that juxtaposition: the border town of Columbus, New Mexico.

Columbus has burned itself into my mind ever since I first visited family there many years ago. Like many border towns, it can look bleak, a place for outsiders and the disenfranchised. But it is in fact a place where great beauty and strength exist alongside harsh realities. I knew then, and each time I returned afterward, that someday I would write a story set in Columbus, much like Paulo knew someday he would make a movie of when he first met Dani. It was only in this place that I could imagine Dani meeting people like Paulo and his grandmother, who have lived through unspeakable tragedy but find strength to go on. And kids like Jessie and Chicken and Yolanda, who understand what it is to be seen as an outsider, to be openly disparaged, and who live on the fringes of a society that doesn't seem to care about them, but who still dare to hope and dream. This setting, those who live there and who offered their wisdom, friendship, and aid to Dani, were essential in her journey.

There is power in seeing and knowing that even if we are locked in a self-made prison, as Meursault is, as humans, we don't have to stay there. The only inescapable prisons are the ones we lock ourselves in. Yes, there are bears walking this earth and waiting for us even before we are pushed out of our mothers' wombs. But we *can* fight the bear, whoever or whatever it may be. We can strengthen ourselves, create new families and relationships.

We can hope.

ACKNOWLEDGMENTS

My deepest and sincerest thanks to:

Kerry Sparks and the whole team at Levine Greenberg Rostan, who continue to be so incredibly supportive of my work.

Beverly Horowitz for knowing what this book needed to be, and everyone at Delacorte Press/Penguin Random House who helped it make its way into the world.

Mr. Halback, because you introduced Meursault to a bunch of jaded teenagers back in the day. And everyone in that senior English class (especially, especially Kris Trego!) because we met Meursault together. I can still see us as we were in that classroom, stumbling through life, trying to figure out the world and find our place in it.

Lauren Gibaldi Mathur and Jessica Low Martinez,

because you are amazing writers and the dearest friends. And because when I said I was writing a story with an opening scene of a bear mauling, you both grinned perfectly and said, "Yes . . . do it!" Also, because "It's never over. . . ."

Susan Frith, because of conversations and coffee and tea and characters standing over our shoulders demanding our attention.

Mami, Papi, Nancy, y David, lo que es ser familia, verdad? Viejitos, cuando pienso las tierras que viajaron, peligrosas y lindas, para encontrarse, me quedo sin palabras. Y como nosotros nacimos de ustedes. Es un gran misterio, un milagro, como se juntaron todas nuestras almas. Solo Dios sabrá. Pero doy gracias. Que lindo compartir esta vida con ustedes. Como los quiero.

Martha y Trinidad Sanchez por enseñarme la belleza del desierto. Suegra, usted especialmente por compartir su cariño y los tésitos que curan tanto.

Ava and Mateo and Francesca, because of car rides and sun-drenched streets and orange soda and music so loud we dance in our seats and open windows to let in hot breezes and you three, you three, with me always, feeling so good. Feeling so cool.

Nando, because you see what I can't and you tell me until I believe and you make what always seems out of reach seem possible. Because of fireworks and sad nights on coffee shop patios. Because of flowers you let be and mariachis and the old man singing. And because . . . infinitely because.

And finally, forever, Patti Magee, because of 1994, high school, and you with your poetry readings and dimmed classroom full of so many words and ideas. Your voice leading us, giving us confidence and making us feel like we mattered. I found my way to you in college, and years later, to the English department where it was one of my greatest privileges to teach with you. I hope you know how much you made me love literature and wonder about everything, everything, and how much you taught me, and what a hand you had in making me the person I am. I hope you are somewhere reciting Blake's "The Tyger" and making the universe answer. I will miss you. I hope your spirit is in every forest, in every tree, in every place you ever camped and sought and just were and every place you wished to go. I hope you made it to Alaska. O Captain!

ABOUT THE AUTHOR

JENNY TORRES SANCHEZ is a full-time writer and former English teacher. She was born in Brooklyn, New York, but has lived on the border of two worlds her whole life. She lives in Orlando, Florida, with her husband and their children. *Because of the Sun* is her third novel. Visit her online at jennytorressanchez.com and on Facebook and follow her on Twitter at @jetchez.